# A Murder
# Too Many

## By E. X. Ferrars

# E. X. FERRARS

# A Murder
# Too Many

**Doubleday**
NEW YORK LONDON TORONTO SYDNEY AUCKLAND

All of the characters in this book are fictitious, and any resemblance to actual persons, living or dead, is purely coincidental.

Published by Doubleday, a division of Bantam Doubleday Dell Publishing Group, Inc. 666 Fifth Avenue, New York, New York 10103

DOUBLEDAY and the portrayal of an anchor with a dolphin are trademarks of Doubleday, a division of Bantam Doubleday Dell Publishing Group, Inc.

Library of Congress Cataloging-in-Publication Data

Ferrars, E. X.
  A murder too many.

  I. Title.
PR6003.R458M84   1988      823'.912      88-11856
ISBN 0-385-24611-0

BG

# A Murder
# Too Many

# One

THE TRAIN came to a standstill beside the gasworks, about a quarter of a mile short of the station of Knotlington, as it always had, all those years ago when Professor Andrew Basnett, F.R.S., had been the youngest of Assistant Lecturers in the Department of Botany at Knotlington University. But some things do not change.

He knew that the train would stay where it was for about three minutes, then potter slowly on into the station. Sitting and waiting, he found it amusing to discover that he felt almost a kind of affection for the great grey cylinders. They seemed to symbolize the beginning of his career, a career that on the whole he had enjoyed. It had taken him from Assistant Lecturer to Lecturer, then Senior Lecturer, then Reader, then on to a Chair in the college in London University where many years before he had taken his degree. He had remained in that Chair, living

in a pleasant flat in St. John's Wood, until his retirement five
years ago.

He lived in the flat alone now, because Nell, his wife, who had
accompanied him step by step as he moved up the academic
ladder, had died of cancer ten years before. In those ten years he
had grown used, after a fashion, to solitariness, but now, looking
out at the gasworks, an ugly scar on a scene that had all too
many ugly scars on it, he had a sudden very clear memory of
how he and Nell had first arrived here together and how the
train had stopped at this very spot. Nell, who had grown up in
the soft green of Hampshire, had never before been in one of
England's big industrial cities, or known anything of their grimness, and there had been a trace of dismay in her voice as she
exclaimed, "Well, here we are!"

Since leaving Knotlington, Andrew had returned to it a number of times. He had come to conferences and to give the occasional lecture and to act as External Examiner in the department of which he had once been the most junior member. But
he found that department hardly recognisable now. It had been
entirely rebuilt, with an amount of money spent on it that
would have seemed the most improbable of daydreams to the
people who had worked there in those long-ago days—people
who, even if they had not drifted on, as he had done, to other
universities, were by now either dead or, like himself, retired.
He found no familiar faces in his old department when he returned to it.

He was acquainted with the present Professor of Botany, Walter Greenslade, but that was because Walter had been a student
of Andrew's in his London University days. He also had one or
two other friends in the town, which had changed in general as
much as the university had. Since the war much of its ancient
grime had been removed, and buildings which had once been
mere black, flat, faceless blocks had been revealed, after cleaning, as charming and well-proportioned Georgian houses. The
trams that had once screeched along the streets had gone, and a

good deal of the smoke that had once belched from the many
chimneys in the town had been compulsorily reduced. But the
gasworks were unaltered, and so was the little pause for breath
that the train gave when it came abreast of them. It filled Andrew for a moment with a sad but quite pleasant nostalgia.

He had changed a good deal himself with the passing years.
He was a tall man, but recently he had acquired a habit of stoop-
ing slightly which made him seem to have shrunk. He was lean
and had bony features, short grey hair, and grey eyes under
eyebrows that were still strikingly dark. His long sight was still
good and he needed glasses only for reading. There had always
been a look of good nature about him, but this was blended now
with a trace of vagueness, as if he sometimes caught himself
wondering where he was and why he was there. He was coming
to Knotlington now to attend a conference of the Botanical Association, a society of which he had once been Secretary, before
his elevation to a Chair.

He was not sure why he was coming. He was still a member
of the Association, paying his yearly subscription faithfully,
even if, when this went up, he sometimes forgot to change his
banker's order. But he had had very little to do with the society
for many years. However, when he had received the usual notifi-
cation of the conference to be held in Knotlington in July some
impulse had moved him for once to attend it. There was a possibility, he had thought, that he would meet some old colleagues,
which would probably be enjoyable, and he might even find
something stimulating in contact with the younger members of
his profession. And then there had been the letter that he had
received from Giles Farmoor. An odd letter.

Not that the letter by itself would have brought Andrew to
Knotlington. He knew that Giles was an odd person, not always
to be taken seriously. His occasional letters had a way of seem-
ing to say more than he actually put into words. Even in the
chats on the telephone, to which he was addicted, or over a quiet
lunch, he often gave the impression of keeping to himself mat-

ters which it would be a grave breach of confidence to discuss. But the last letter that Andrew had had from him had been relatively explicit, urging him to come to the conference of the Botanical Association because this would provide excellent cover for his visit, and incidentally, because Giles was in need of advice from someone he trusted.

The suggestion that Andrew might be in need of cover if he chose to visit Knotlington had of course been merely flippant, and it had entertained him as well as stimulating his curiosity, thus helping to promote a feeling that after all it was worth his while from time to time to encounter other scientists and not accept a view of himself, which had been developing in him lately, that he was firmly and irrevocably lodged on the shelf. Anyway, here he was, looking at the gasworks.

The time was four-fifteen and he was not to meet Giles Farmoor until dinner that evening. In the interval he went to the room that had been reserved for him in one of the student hostels, empty of students at present since the long vacation had begun. The one in which he found himself lodged had been built long after he had moved on from the town. It was a pleasant, square building, faced with grey stone and surrounded by lawns and flowering trees and rose beds, at present richly flushed with bloom. A high stone wall surrounded the grounds. The room allotted to Andrew had light-coloured furniture, a dark brown carpet, pale green curtains, and a quantity of paperbacks in a bookshelf. When Andrew looked at these he saw that they were mostly detective stories and science fiction, which ought to indicate, he thought, though perhaps it did not, that the student whose room it was was a serious character who had taken what scholarly work he possessed home with him to study in the vacation, leaving his escapist literature behind. On a writing table under a window there was an envelope with Andrew's name on it.

He opened it and found a note from Professor Greenslade, inviting him to join him for a drink in the staff club at six

o'clock. In Andrew's time in Knotlington there had been no
such thing as a staff club, but at a later date one had come into
existence—a slim, modern structure between two solid, smoke-
stained Victorian buildings. He knew his way to it and as the
summer evening was fine he decided to walk. It would probably
take him no longer than going by bus, as the traffic in the home-
going rush hour was very congested, moving very slowly from
one set of lights to the next. Besides the thick flow of private
cars making for the suburbs, big lorries went lumbering past,
their engines roaring, their brakes squealing. Andrew felt
thankful that the room that he had been given in the hostel was
at the back of it, so that if this kind of noise continued into the
night it was unlikely to disturb him.

The staff club was in a side street which was lined on both
sides with parked cars, but led nowhere and so at least was
quiet. Inside there was a long lounge with a bar at the far end of
it. Walter Greenslade was at the bar and at the moment appeared to be having an argument with someone, a not very ami-
cable argument. He was irritably contradicting something that
had just been said to him. He had a carrying voice and was
saying, "I don't agree with you. Not at all! It's high time we got
rid of the bloody things."

There was a quiet hum of talk in the place. Along one side of
it were three tall windows which gave a not very interesting
view of a blank wall outside, which belonged to the neighbour-
ing building. On the wall of the lounge between the windows
hung a row of pictures which Andrew did not remember having
seen there before. They were mostly portraits and caught his
eye in a way that made him think that presently he would take a
more thoughtful look at them. But for the moment his object
was to join Walter Greenslade.

He was sitting on a stool by the bar, with one elbow resting
on it and with what looked like a very strong whisky and soda in
his hand. That surprised Andrew, for Walter had always been
an abstemious man. But the whisky was not the only surprise

that Andrew's first glance at Walter gave him. In the four years since they had last happened to meet at a Royal Society conversazione Walter had changed very much. His rather long, bland, smooth face was not merely far more sallow than it had been then, but was positively haggard. His grey eyes behind metal-rimmed spectacles looked sunken and had a nervous gleam in them instead of the slightly smug calm that Andrew remembered. In a moment of intuition of the kind that sometimes occurs in the very first glimpse that one has of someone whom one has not seen for some time, and which will fade as soon as familiar expressions and gestures reappear, Andrew thought with some distress that he was looking at a very sick man, a man almost on the edge of a breakdown.

If Walter had not been in a group of people, some of whom, like Andrew, had presumably come to the conference of the Botanical Association, he would probably have asked Walter straight away what was wrong. But that could hardly be done when he was apparently playing host to the people round him. And seeing Andrew approach his face brightened. He got down from his stool, clapped Andrew on the shoulder, asked if he had had a good journey, was the room that they had given him comfortable, and what would he like to drink.

Then he gestured at the people round him and said, "I expect you all know each other."

His voice was attractive, mellow and soft and intimate. As soon as Andrew had the sherry for which he had asked, and the other members of the group around the bar were occupied with one another, Walter took Andrew by the arm and drew him closer.

"Did you notice all those pictures along there as you came in?" he asked. "I was just having an argument about them with some of these people. I'm always being told they're genius, but to me they're hideous, almost obscene, as well as just damned incompetent. Genius my foot! They've only been hung there out of sentiment. The man was a member of the University and

he happened to get himself murdered, and there they'll hang in
memory of him to all eternity as far as I can see. I've tried telling
people that enough is enough and it's time they were taken
down and dumped somewhere well out of sight. But nobody
listens to me. Best artist there's been in Knotlington this century, I'm told. But I just find them plain offensive. I'm sure
Knotlington's got some other artists it wouldn't do any harm for
the club to patronize. Now tell me honestly, what do you think
of them?"

Andrew would have gone to take a look at one or two of the
pictures if Walter had not held him so firmly by the arm.

"Who was the artist?" Andrew asked.

"Fellow called Judd—Carl Judd," Walter answered.

The name rang a bell faintly in Andrew's memory.

"And you said he was murdered?" he asked. "Ah yes, he was
on the staff here, wasn't he? I remember reading about it now. I
was abroad at the time in Australia, and there was some shemoz-
zle going on in the Middle East too which probably was going to
mean a war, so I didn't pay much attention to what was happening here. In fact, I only noticed it because it had happened in
Knotlington. What department was he in?"

"Fine Arts," Walter said. "He was a lecturer. Useless in his
job because he couldn't be bothered with students. Other people's wives were more his line."

Walter himself was unmarried, so his apparent bias against
the dead lecturer could not have been caused by his having
taken an undue interest in a wife of Walter's.

"It was about two years ago it happened, wasn't it?" Andrew
said.

"Just about."

"He was beaten up and strangled, I seem to remember."

"No, stabbed."

"Ah yes. And they never got who did it, did they?"

"Oh yes, it was a chap called Stephen Sharland, in the Botany
Department. You mean you really don't remember it?" Walter

Greenslade looked astonished. "He got life. And Judd's place
has been taken by a harmless little white mouse of a man. Well, I
say harmless, but it's he who got the club committee to hang all
those pictures there. Got hold of them from Margaret Judd and
when they were first hung it was supposed to be just for an
exhibition in memory of the man. But we seem to be stuck with
them for good. They've already been there for months. But why
are we talking about the things? It's just that I get irritated by
them every time I come in here. You'll join us for dinner, won't
you?"

Andrew replied that he had already arranged to have dinner
with Giles Farmoor.

"A pity," Walter said. "Well, how have things been going with
you? How's the book getting along?"

It always embarrassed Andrew to be asked about his book.
Soon after his retirement he had started to write a life of Robert
Hooke, the noted seventeenth-century microscopist, botanist,
and architect. In those days people had not been drilled into
specialization as they are in modern times, and it had been possible to be both a scientist and an artist at the same time. This
quality in the man had always had a fascination for Andrew,
and as he believed that there were some papers relating to
Hooke in the library of the university here he was hoping to be
able to spend some time studying them instead of attending all
the lectures in the conference programme.

But he preferred not to discuss his work. The trouble with it
was that over the years it never seemed to grow any longer. It
absorbed him. He spent hours on it. But a good many of those
hours were spent in destroying what he had written the day
before, and he had an uneasy feeling that a number of the people
who knew him well probably thought of his endeavours as a
joke. Of course they were polite about it. They asked him how it
was coming along and appeared to take it seriously, but as he
sometimes was himself in discouraged moods, they were probably quite sure that it would never be finished. When he was

directly questioned about it, however, he always said that it was progressing well, then did his best to change the subject.

This happened to be made easy now because a small man suddenly appeared at Andrew's elbow and said, "You must be Professor Basnett."

Andrew had no memory of ever having seen the man before, but Walter introduced him as the university registrar, Kenneth Marriott, and the little man assured Andrew that he had attended lectures of his many years ago. He looked about fifty, was rather portly, and had a round, long face with plump cheeks, slightly protuberant brown eyes like a spaniel's, and a high, smooth forehead. He told Andrew that although he had taken a degree in biology, he had long ago found out that he had no aptitude for science and had drifted into administration. He had been in Knotlington for five years.

"But I can't add much to what Walter was telling you about our great scandal here," he said cheerfully, giving Walter a dig in the ribs and grinning up at him. "The Sharland calamity. I know that's what you were talking about, wasn't it, Walter? Why can't you forget it? Brush it under the carpet, as most of us seem to have been able to do."

"I suppose because Sharland was in my own department," Walter said. "I knew him quite well, or thought I did, and I used to believe he had quite a future."

Kenneth Marriott turned back to Andrew. "What do you think of Judd's paintings yourself, Professor Basnett?"

"I haven't really looked at them yet," Andrew answered.

"Well, come along then." Marriott drew Andrew away from Walter Greenslade's grasp and led him up to one of the paintings on the opposite wall.

It was of a woman washing dishes at a sink. She was in jeans and a sack-like sweater and had yellow hair tied back in a pony-tail. The colours were muddy except for the yellow hair, and the picture did not particularly appeal to Andrew though he recognised in it a crude sort of strength which, for all he knew, might

indicate genius or something like it. But he was the last person
to set himself up as any kind of judge.

"Doesn't impress you," the small man said after a moment.

Andrew did not reply but strolled on to the next picture in
the line on the wall.

It was mud-coloured too and seemed to be of the same
woman, though this time she was in a mechanic's overall and
was doing something under the raised bonnet of a car.

"Seems to be a hard worker," he said. "Who is she?"

"The woman?" Marriott said. "Judd's wife, though it hardly
does her justice. She's quite a looker."

"Does she still live here?"

"Yes, she stayed on in the house where it happened."

"Was she about at the time?"

"Not in the house. She belongs to some choir and was at a
rehearsal they were having. But she found the body, and she
found something else that surprised people. Judd had been doing a portrait of Veronica Greenslade, Walter's sister, and it had
been slashed from top to bottom. And it had been done with the
same knife that had just been used to kill Judd. There were
blood stains on the canvas that were certainly the same group as
his and made when the blood on the knife must have been quite
fresh."

"What happened to the knife?"

"It was never found."

"What was Judd doing, painting Veronica Greenslade's portrait, if Walter always disliked his work as much as he does
now?"

"That's one of the questions that's never been answered.
Come along, see what you think of some of the others."

By the time they returned to the group at the bar Andrew
found that Walter Greenslade had dropped the subject of Judd's
paintings and was discussing the venation of the leaf with a
young man from Glasgow University whom he held by the arm
and who was to read a paper on the subject the next day. An-

drew chatted for a while with a former colleague, who as a matter of fact he had always disliked, then returned to take a look on his own at some more of the murdered man's pictures.

He was looking at one, which he concluded was a landscape because there were some recognisable trees in the background, though there were some disconnected wheels and human faces in the foreground, and he was wondering why it gave him the sense of power that it did, when Giles Farmoor came hurriedly in at the swing doors and rushed to Andrew's side.

"I'm late—I'm sorry," Giles said. "I got caught on a job I didn't expect. I've been cutting up a prostitute who got herself strangled by one of her customers. Quite straightforward case. I really needn't have been called in at all. And those damned police didn't even offer me a drink when I'd finished. Have you had a drink? I could do with one myself, if you don't mind." He glanced towards the bar. "But we don't want to get involved with that gang. What will you have? Whisky? That's what I feel like myself."

Andrew chose another sherry and Giles Farmoor went charging off to the bar, diving with some fierceness through the throng of people who clustered around it, quickly obtaining what he wanted and returning to Andrew with two drinks in his hands.

Suggesting then that they should sit down at a table at the far end of the lounge, he guided Andrew to one that had just been vacated by a young couple, and said, "Well, it's good to see you."

Giles, who had trained in plant physiology, had long ago moved out of that field into forensic science and from what he had said on joining Andrew, had presumably been spending his afternoon performimg a post mortem on a murdered prostitute. Andrew always found it difficult to connect him with the kind of work that he did. Giles was a slender fine-boned man, not as tall as Andrew, with a narrow, thoughtful, sensitive face that might have belonged to someone engaged in some highly esoteric form of scholarship, rather than to someone who could

take the cutting up of dead bodies in his stride. He had thick
brown hair which stood up in two peaks above his rather promi-
nent ears. His eyes were brown and there was a general look of
brownness about him, which came partly from the freckles that
speckled his creamy skin and partly from his liking for neat
brown suits, pale brown shirts, brown ties and brown shoes. He
was a little older than Walter Greenslade but looked far
younger.

He sat down, swallowed most of his whisky at a gulp and said,
"Ah, that's good. Those morgues are so bloody cold. You're
looking very well, Andrew. How's the book coming along?"

Andrew gave his usual false sort of reply. "Reasonably. Quite
reasonably. I believe there are some papers in the library here
that I might find interesting. I'll see if I can fix up to get a look
at them tomorrow. They're partly why I came, you know. I
don't come to many of these sorts of things nowadays. I feel I'm
just a ghost out of the past, I've lost touch with nearly everything that's going on. But you wanted me to come, didn't you,
Giles? You said something in your letter about wanting my advice. That was nonsense, of course. Listening to someone else's
advice, as I'm sure you know, is one of the surest ways of making a mess of things. The only times I've ever listened to advice,
it's always been disastrous. You must have had the same experience."

"I suppose I have," Giles said. "And that may be why I
thought I'd like a talk with you. You won't dream of giving me
any advice. I can feel quite safe about that. But you may prod
me into making up my own mind about what I ought to do.
That's always useful."

"At least you won't be able to blame me then if it turns out
you've done the wrong thing."

Giles took his narrow brown face between his hands, resting
his elbows on his knees and looking at Andrew apparently intently. Yet there was an almost secretive expression in his eyes

which Andrew knew and which suggested that Giles did not really intend to say much about what was on his mind.

"Oh well, we'll talk about it some other time," he said. "But tell me something. You've had some experience of murder, haven't you?"

"My God!" Andrew exclaimed in sharp exasperation. "Is that why you got me here? *No!* No, I haven't! Well, all right, I have, but entirely by mistake. It isn't one of my interests."

"Sorry, sorry," Giles said. "We'll talk about something else."

"People in this hole *can* talk about something else, can they?" Andrew said. "I've heard nothing else but murder since I got here."

"You must admit it's one of the things that's brought Knotlington University more into the public eye than anything else that's happened here for a long time," Giles said. "It rocked the academic world to its foundations. However, if you'd sooner talk about something different, there's something you might tell me. How does Greenslade strike you?"

"Walter?" Andrew said. "As a matter of fact, I was going to ask you about that. I've only had a short chat with him this evening, but it started me wondering what was the matter with him. He's changed very much since I saw him last. He used to be a placid sort of chap, always very sure of himself, but now he looks nervous and ill. I even wondered if he was on the edge of a breakdown of some kind. Is that what you wanted to know?"

Giles nodded, but said nothing.

"Is it the general view of him here?" Andrew asked.

"I don't really know," Giles said. "I think he's getting a reputation for being difficult and unreliable, which isn't doing him any good. But I remembered that you and he are friends and I thought you might be able to help."

"He really needs help, does he? It isn't just some temporary thing?"

"I think it's been going on for some time. I believe it dates

back to when his sister died, though I didn't notice it for some
time after that."

"Veronica's dead? I didn't know that." It shook Andrew that
he should not have known it, even if he would not have described Walter and himself as close friends. But they had known
each other for a great many years, had always had sufficiently
pleasant relations and shared many interests. "What happened
to her?"

"She took an overdose of sodium amytal. She did it when
Walter was away somewhere and he came home and found her
when she'd been dead several days. God knows how many
grains she took, with half a bottle of whisky. Luckily for me I
didn't have to do the post mortem, as I was fairly involved with
the family."

"Good lord, how awful!" Though why death, chosen deliberately, should seem any worse than natural death, probably unde-
sired, Andrew could not have said. "Why did she do it? Does
anyone know?"

"Oh, there was lots of talk about it at the time, of course. She
was supposed to have been involved with Judd, for one thing,
and he was known for treating his women fairly brutally. The
story that went round was that she'd thought he was going to
leave his wife for her and killed herself when she found he
hadn't the least intention of doing so."

"Then was it Veronica's death that's turned Walter so vio-
lently against Judd, even after all this time?"

"Quite likely, I should think."

"I only met her two or three times. She and Walter lived
together, didn't they? I remember I used to think that it was one
of those over-close relationships between a brother and sister
that did neither of them any good, probably only just stopping
short of actual incest. Somehow I felt it stopped Walter from
ever becoming fully mature. Did her suicide happen before
Judd's murder or after it?"

"About three weeks before."

"It seems a weird question to ask, Giles, but was Walter ever suspected of the murder?"

"Oh, of course. But so was Judd's wife. He'd been doing a portrait of Veronica at the time it happened, and someone, whether or not it was the murderer we don't know, pulled out the knife that had been used to kill Judd and slashed the portrait with it."

"So that little man, Marriott, was telling me."

"It naturally suggested jealousy. But if Walter was guilty I suppose you'd say the motive was revenge, because he thought Judd had driven Veronica to kill herself. Anyway, they got pretty conclusive evidence against Sharland and he's doing life for it."

"Now look here," Andrew said, "you wanted me to come here for some reason and it wasn't simply because you want me somehow to prop up poor old Walter. There's something else behind it, so why don't you come out into the open and tell me what it is? It's what you'll do in the end, so why not get on with it?"

A flicker of uncertainty appeared in Giles's brown eyes. He drank some of his whisky, frowned down into his glass, looked up again and said hesitantly, "Well, the fact of the matter is . . ."

But at that moment he was interrupted by the appearance of Kenneth Marriott, who said cheerfully, "Mind if I join you?"

Without waiting to be told whether or not he was welcome, the little man sat down at the table. It appeared that he was not having dinner with Walter Greenslade and his guests. They were drifting now from the bar in twos and threes towards the club's restaurant.

"I believe your lot are having a dinner here tomorrow evening," the little registrar said to Andrew. "You'll be going to it, I suppose."

"I suppose so," Andrew answered, though the fact that there

was to be a dinner here the next evening had not really regis-
tered in his mind. "No speeches, I hope."

"I believe not. Not that I'd have to suffer them myself. It's an
affair strictly for you scientific blokes who've assembled here.
Not that it hasn't involved me in a bit of organizing. These
things always do. But I'm off for my own holiday next weekend,
on a Swan's Tour to Greece. It'll be pretty hot at this time of
year, I believe, but I shall enjoy that."

He went on to chat about his plans for his holiday, which it
sounded as if he was taking alone. He made no mention of a wife
or of any friend who would be going with him. Andrew listened
with impatience, wanting to return to the question that Giles
had seemed almost about to answer when Kenneth Marriott had
joined them. But after a few minutes Andrew found that he had
half-forgotten what the question had been. It had been something to do with Giles's real reason for being anxious that Andrew should attend the conference of the Botanical Association
in Knotlington.

But did it matter after all what that reason had been? It was
not what had brought Andrew here. He had come because he
had had a feeling that he should really not allow himself to drift
completely out of touch with what was going forward in his
own subject, and because he had been told about the papers
relating to Robert Hooke which were said to be in the library
here.

"By the way," he said, interrupting Marriott in a description
of the cultural pleasures to be enjoyed on a Swan's tour, "do you
know a man called Ramsden—Gregory Ramsden?"

"Greg?" Marriott said. "Our librarian. Yes, of course I know
him."

"I'd like to get in touch with him tomorrow," Andrew said.
"What's the best way for me to do that? Should I telephone
him?"

"I'd just go into the library and introduce yourself," Marriott said. "A very interesting fellow, you'll find, and very easy to get on with. You'll like him . . ."

"Look," Giles broke in, "there she is."

Marriott gave a violent start and stopped in midsentence. After one swift glance over his shoulder he seemed to shrink into himself, drawing his shoulders up to his ears, almost as if he were trying to hide himself from someone inside his own small, plump body. The person whose presence he seemed desperately anxious at all costs not to have to acknowledge was a tall woman who had just come in at the swing doors. She stood still for a moment inside the doors, then walked towards the bar, which at the moment was deserted. It seemed to Andrew that as she passed a curious silence fell on the groups still gathered around the tables spaced throughout the room, and that the people at each table then began hastily talking again in slightly raised voices, as if to conceal the fact that they had noticed her.

She was a tall woman of about thirty with a bony, angular sort of grace. She had a pale, pointed face and fair hair, cut short and falling in a soft swirl across her forehead. She wore a high-necked dress of ivory silk with a green brooch that might have been real jade on one shoulder. She had a striking yet unself-conscious elegance, and she looked at no one as she passed by.

"Oh God, why does she do it?" Marriott said in a half-whisper. "Why *will* she do it?"

The woman had gone to the bar and was ordering a drink for herself.

Giles explained it to Andrew. "That's Gwen Sharland. She comes in every evening just about now, has a drink by herself, stays a few minutes, then goes away. It's atrociously sad really."

"And she isn't even a member of the club," Marriott groaned. "Why doesn't someone stop her? The porter ought not to allow her in."

"Stop her yourself," Giles suggested.

"You know I couldn't do that." Marriott looked shocked. "I'm just about the last person who could."

"You see, it's her way of asserting to all of us here that she believes in her husband's innocence," Giles told Andrew. "She never says anything about it. It's just the way she's chosen of demonstrating her faith in him."

Marriott rose hurriedly to his feet.

"Look, I'm going," he said, still in a tensely lowered voice. "I can't stand seeing her. Hope to see you again, Professor Basnett, while you're here. Good evening."

He went rapidly to the door.

"He seems remarkably upset," Andrew observed.

"It's only natural. He was the main witness against Sharland."

The woman swallowed her drink quickly, turned and walked swiftly back to the entrance. As she went her eyes dwelt for a moment on Andrew's face, but did not appear to see him. He noticed, however, what an unusual shade of green they were. Most eyes that are called green are really grey with only a tinge of green in them, but hers were hardly less truly green the jade that she wore.

"Lovely, isn't she?" Giles said with a note of sombre detachment in his voice as if he were looking at something beautiful that had somehow been hopelessly ruined.

"And you agree with her, don't you?" Andrew said. "That's really why you wanted me to come here. You believe in Sharland's innocence and you want me to help you decide what you ought to do about it."

# TWO

GILES DID NOT DENY IT. He only gave Andrew a thoughtful look, then suggested that they should go in to dinner. They finished their drinks and went into the restaurant, where they saw Walter and his guests seated at a long table at one end of the room. Choosing a small table at the other end, they ordered steaks and a carafe of red wine which Giles warned Andrew would not be distinguished, then sat in a silence that was curiously uneasy until their food arrived.

Perhaps because Andrew had not attempted to obtain any answer to his question, Giles at last spoke with a slightly resentful abruptness.

"All right, yes. That is, no. Or perhaps I ought to say that I've been wanting someone to talk the thing over with, but not because I'm convinced Sharland's innocent. It's just the possibility that he *might* be, which I find is enough to keep me awake at night. Of course I always liked the man and I suppose that's my only reason for finding it almost impossible to believe in his guilt."

"Quite a good reason," Andrew said. "But of course it isn't evidence. I suppose there are people who don't like him."

"Not many," Giles replied. "He was popular on the whole. The verdict came as a shock to a lot of us."

"But not to that little man we've been talking to."

Giles crumbled some bread on his side-plate, looking down frowningly at his fingers.

"I'm not sure about that. I'm not sure it wasn't worse for him than for most of us," he said. "Marriott's a curious character. It's obvious he hates himself for having given the evidence that convicted Sharland."

"What was it?"

It took Giles some time to make up his mind to reply. Andrew thought that he was going to withdraw into one of his moods of wary reticence. But after a moment he said, "He saw Sharland come out of Judd's house at about the relevant time with blood on the pullover he was wearing. Of course Marriott wasn't sure it was blood. It was about eleven o'clock in the evening and it was dark, but the lamps along the street were bright and he could see dark stains on the pullover, which was a light grey. And when he told the police about the stains they went to look for the pullover, and it was bundled up in a drawer in the Sharlands' flat and the stains were blood and it was the same group as Judd's."

"What was Marriott doing, passing the Judds' house at eleven in the evening?" Andrew asked.

"He was on his way home from dinner with the Vice-Chancellor. Marriott lived quite close to the Judds and he was passing their house when he saw Sharland come out. As Marriott's described it, Sharland slammed the front door shut behind him and went running to where his car was parked in the street. At the time Marriott was puzzled, with a sort of feeling that something was wrong, but he didn't really worry about it till he

heard next day that Judd had been found dead, with a number of
stab wounds in his neck and chest."

"And he went to the police then?"

"I think they came to him. There'd been someone else on the
other side of the street when Sharland came out of the house
who'd seen Marriott as well as Sharland. A neighbour of Judd's,
who didn't know either Marriott or Sharland. But this man described them, and the police came round to Marriott and when
he told them about what had looked like stains on Sharland's
pullover they went to his house and found the pullover with the
blood on it. And not long after he was charged with murder."

"What was his motive supposed to have been?"

"The usual one, when Judd was involved. A woman."

"Sharland's wife?"

Giles nodded.

Andrew sipped some of the wine which Giles had accurately
warned him was not distinguished.

"That woman we saw at the bar," he said.

Giles nodded again.

"Then what d'you make of her daily protest that her husband's innocent?" Andrew asked.

"It could be a protest that she's innocent herself, couldn't it?"
Giles crumbled some more bread, frowning at some thought
that was passing through his mind. "Judd was one of those men
who get themselves reputations for being virtually irresistible
where women are concerned. Some women, anyway. The kind
who are looking for someone over-sexed with more than a bit of
the satyr about him. Judd even had a bit of a look of the satyr,
rather big pointed ears, slightly goat-like features, and a sort of
assertion of excessive virility. I was never altogether convinced
by it myself. It's a type, as often as not, I'm inclined to think,
that's really unsure under the surface of being genuinely able to
satisfy a woman."

"That woman, Mrs. Sharland, whom we saw, was she one of
the kind who'd have been attracted by him?"

"It's possible."

"Do you know her well?"

Giles shook his head. "Not really. I used to see a fair amount of the Judds and the Sharlands before the murder and it never occurred to me that there was anything between Gwen Sharland and Judd. If there was anything, I think it was something quite trivial, and I don't think Sharland's the irrationally jealous sort of man who'd have worked himself up to doing murder on account of it."

"So the only evidence against him is that Marriott saw him come out of the house at what you called the relevant time, and the blood on his pullover."

"That's just about it."

"What was the relevant time?"

"As I told you, it was a little after eleven that Marriott saw him. And Judd and Margaret, his wife, had had dinner together at eight o'clock, then she'd gone out to a rehearsal of a choir she belongs to and got home at about eleven-thirty. She found Judd murdered, called the police at once and they decided he'd been dead for half an hour to an hour before she found him. But of course you know how uncertain that can be. She really hadn't an alibi. But when they questioned Sharland next day about what he'd been doing in the house the evening before, he said he'd gone in to discuss the possibility that Judd might do a portrait of Gwen. He said he'd found the front door unlatched, got no answer when he rang, went in and found Judd in his studio, stabbed, with a lot of blood on him. Sharland said that was how he got the blood on himself. He'd thought there was a possibility Judd wasn't dead and tried to turn him over to see just what had happened, then suddenly he lost his nerve and panicked and rushed out. One of his problems was that he and Judd had had a quarrel a few days before because of something Sharland had said about one of Judd's paintings, actually a painting of Veronica Greenslade, and he said his idea of asking Judd to paint

Gwen was partly to try to make it up with him. Unfortunately for him, he wasn't believed."

"Did you believe him?"

Giles hesitated for so long that Andrew felt fairly certain that what he would eventually be told would not be the truth. Yet when Giles spoke there was an air of cautious accuracy about what he said.

"Yes, I believed him. I had to, or else I had to accept the probability that what had taken Sharland into Judd's house was an intention to do murder."

"You don't sound as if you're altogether convinced by your own argument."

"Perhaps I'm not."

"Look, Giles," Andrew said, "if your reason for wanting me to come here was something to do with getting Sharland cleared of killing Judd, hadn't you better be a little less cautious with me? If you're sure Sharland's innocent, I'm quite ready to assume you're right. But that's only because I've a considerable trust in your judgement. I know nothing about this crime. And remember, I know very little about crime in general, even if I've got involved with it once or twice. So if you want me to help you in some way—and just how you think I can is something that puzzles me somewhat—you'll have to come more into the open with me. Why do you really think Sharland went into Judd's house that evening?"

Giles gave a sigh, shifted uneasily in his chair, then turned his attention not very enthusiastically to his steak. After a moment he said, "I don't believe it's so very important."

"You mean he might have dropped in any evening, perhaps was even in the habit of doing it, and that evening he just happened to be so unlucky as to walk in on a murder?"

"Does that sound so very improbable to you?"

"Not really. I suppose it could easily have happened. This quarrel that he and Judd had about Veronica's portrait, do you know what it was all about?"

"I think Sharland was a bit more critical than Judd was inclined to tolerate," Giles answered. "He didn't take kindly to
criticism."

"And that was all? Judd's relationship with Sharland's wife
didn't come into it?"

"Not so far as I know."

Andrew thought of how often in the past work of his own had
been criticized in ways that had roused bitter anger in him,
anger that perhaps had gone beyond the fringe of mere bitterness into something which at least temporarily had filled him
with an emotion which had felt frighteningly destructive, yet
even at its worst was a long way short of any realistic desire to
do murder. That was something that he had never experienced.

"I suppose it couldn't have been Judd who invited Sharland to
come round to his house so that they could finish their row
about the painting, or possibly about Gwen Sharland, in peace,"
he said. "You say Mrs. Judd was out, Judd was alone. But if he'd
gone on brooding about what Sharland had said about the portrait and the situation in general, he might suddenly have
phoned him and got him to come round so that they could have
the thing out. But tell me now, Giles, what sort of man is Marriott?" Andrew had dealt with his steak and laid down his knife
and fork.

Giles gave him one of his thoughtful, cautious glances.

"It's odd that you should say that," he said.

"Why?"

"Because I was just going to get around to that myself. I was
going to ask you what you made of him."

Andrew sat back in his chair, pondering before making his
reply.

"So he isn't all that he seems to be," he said at length.

"What do you think he seems to be?" Giles asked.

"Oh, pleasant enough. Friendly, moderately intelligent, if not
brilliant, but a good deal more twisted than he wants to make

himself out to be. His reaction to that woman was odd, even if
he thinks he's responsible for having had her husband convicted."

"So his act didn't altogether convince you."

"It's an act, is it?"

"No, I think it's genuine as far as it goes. All the same, I
believe he's less of a nice, comfortable sort of fat little man than
he appears on the surface. I think he's actually a fairly difficult
character. His wife left him three or four years ago, I don't
know why. I don't think it was a case of another man. I think
she simply found him a lot more awkward than you'd think. He
isn't much of a success in his job here. He's always getting
across people and he knows he isn't liked."

"That's somehow the impression I got. But is he the sort of
man who'd simply make up the story of having seen Sharland
come out of Judd's house?"

"I don't see how he could have done that. He was right about
the blood on the pullover, you see. If he hadn't seen it, how
could he have known about it? I suppose someone could have
told him, but that doesn't seem likely."

"No."

To Andrew what seemed likely just then was that Kenneth
Marriott had seen just what he had told the police that he had
and that probably he was right that Stephen Sharland *had* murdered Carl Judd. It would never have occurred to Andrew to
question this if Giles were not as convinced as he seemed to be
that this was not what had happened. Giles was a shrewd, perceptive man and his work in forensic science had brought him
into far more contact with crime than Andrew's work ever had.
If Giles wanted to discuss his problem about Sharland with Andrew, it could not really be because he felt that Andrew knew
even half as much as he did himself about murder.

Later that evening, returning to his room in the students'
hostel, Andrew found himself muttering half-aloud to himself:

*"There is a Reaper, whose name is Death,*
*And, with his sickle keen,*
*He reaps the bearded grain at a breath . . ."*

He tried to stop himself. It was what he considered a bad habit, this way he had of reciting verses to himself, or even, if he was sure that he was alone, of actually saying them aloud, hardly knowing at the time what he was doing. It was something that had begun when he was a child. He had had an infallible memory then for verses, remembering for the rest of his life anything that he had read only two or three times. It was an unfortunate habit because what he had read and enjoyed when he was say nine or ten years old was not what really appealed to him now. Here he was, as he strolled back towards the hostel, murmuring lines of Longfellow, a poet for whom he had not the least regard. If he was not careful, he thought, he might soon find himself descending to *The Song of Hiawatha.*

Why could he not recite to himself some Shakespeare or Milton or Donne, remembering which might give him some real pleasure? But most of what had remained stored in his memory was virtually doggerel, with jingly rhythms which were naturally very easy to memorize. As he walked along the street his lips moved faintly and one or two people he passed appeared to notice this, for they gave him mildly amused glances as he went by.

He went to bed as soon as he reached his room in the hostel, but for some time before he settled down to sleep he read an Eric Ambler that he had found on the bookshelf in the room. In the morning he woke early and made his way to the shower room at the end of the passage, then shaved and got dressed. Before going downstairs for breakfast he opened his suitcase and took out a round box that contained triangular segments of cheddar cheese, done up in foil. It was one of his slightly more eccentric habits to start the day with a small helping of cheese. A few years ago he had somehow been convinced by a friend that the day should be begun with some protein, and though the friend had held that a boiled egg was the right thing with which to start the day, Andrew had decided that cheese was dietetically as satisfactory while being far less troublesome to prepare.

He was faintly ashamed of the habit. Being fortunate in suffering from no allergies, he had a view of himself as someone who could eat anything that was put down before him and could survive without undue distress a lack of what he was used to. Whether in fact—if he was being entertained, say, by hospitable Arabs—he would have been able to eat a sheep's eyeball, he was not sure. He would have done his best, though he would have quailed at the thought. Perhaps it would have been beyond him.

In the refectory, where breakfast was served, there was no one whom Andrew knew. He had coffee and a roll and marmalade, then soon afterwards set out for a short walk towards the Botany Department, where the first lecture of the conference was to be held. But before reaching it he turned into a side-street which would take him, he knew, not to the Botany Department but to the University library. It was without thinking much about what he was doing that he took the turning. The morning was a bright one, or would have been but for a faint smoky haze in the air. As he remembered it, only very occasionally did a really sunny sky hang over the town. Even though the sky was clearer now than it would have been in the old days, it lacked the brilliance of even a London summer sky.

The library took up most of one side of a square, the rest of which was taken up by other university buildings, though none of them were devoted to any of the sciences. These were further on into the town. Round this square there were law, classics, economics, languages, and social sciences, and a whole block given up to administration. The library was a grey stone building, opened only about three years ago, austere in design except for a somewhat pretentious entrance. Andrew had never been in it before. Going in, he stood looking round him, and then approached a counter along one side of the lofty hall, behind which an attractive-looking young woman was sitting.

"Good morning," he said. "I should like to speak to Dr. Ramsden if I can. My name is Basnett, Professor Basnett. I believe you've some papers here I'd like a chance to see. Perhaps you could find out from Dr. Ramsden if that's possible."

The girl gave him a charming smile, said, "I'll find out," and picked up a telephone on the counter before her.

She spoke to someone who seemed to be Gregory Ramsden's secretary, put the telephone down, smiled again and said, "He'll be just a moment. He thinks you must be Professor Basnett who's writing a life of Robert Hooke."

It was a long time since Andrew had been conscious of blushing, but he felt as if he must be doing so now. He could not imagine how Gregory Ramsden could have heard that he was writing a life of Robert Hooke. He supposed that he must have spoken about it to someone who had taken him unfortunately seriously. To be asked by people he knew well how the book was coming along was bad enough, but to find that a complete stranger believed in and was interested in it was altogether too disconcerting.

"Do sit down," the girl said, "he won't keep you a minute."

Wishing that he had not come but seeing a chair beside the counter, Andrew sat down, but almost at once he heard a brisk step behind him and hurriedly stood up to shake hands with a man who said, "Professor Basnett? I'm Gregory Ramsden. I'm so glad to see you."

He looked as if he was in his sixties. He was of medium height, slender, very erect, neatly made, with an oval face and neat, sharp features. He had grey hair that was growing a little thin above his forehead, grey eyes, and a pleasant, open smile that showed good, very white teeth, probably manufactured. He wore a well-cut, dark grey double-breasted suit and very well-polished brown shoes. Everything about him appeared carefully looked after, personable and trim.

"You want to see the Hooke diary, of course," he said. "An interesting thing, even though it isn't Robert Hooke's but only a female relative's. There are references in it to Hooke, however, that I assume are what you want to study. Come along. You'd like a look at it now, I expect."

"Thank you," Andrew said, "if that's convenient. Yes, if there's somewhere I could just sit and take a look at it, I'd be very grateful."

"Of course, of course. It hasn't been in our hands for long, you know. I think you're the first person who's taken an interest in it. It came to us along with the collection of Sir Thomas Barnaby. We haven't made a study yet of how it got into his hands. You'll want to go into that yourself, I expect. Sir Thomas died last year and left us his library."

Walking briskly, the librarian led Andrew along a passage off which on both sides there were alcoves, lined with books, and most of them occupied by people seated at tables, with books and papers spread out before them.

"Now how will this suit you?" Gregory Ramsden asked, pausing at an alcove that was empty. "I'll have the diary sent along to you. And by the way, would you care to have dinner with us this evening? I know my wife would like to meet you. She was once a student of yours, you know. But I'm sorry to say she's a bit of an invalid now and can't get out much. I hope you'll come."

Andrew thanked him and though he had a confused feeling that there was some reason why he should not accept the invitation, found himself doing so and saying how much he would look forward to the evening. It was only after Gregory Ramsden had left him that he remembered that there was a dinner that evening being given by the Botanical Association at which he ought to be present.

He would have explained this regretfully to Ramsden if it had been he who had appeared with the diary, but it was brought to him by a young woman. On the whole the easiest thing to do,

Andrew thought, would be to skip the Botanical dinner at
which he was not likely to be missed. Then, sitting down at the
table in the alcove with the diary and a notebook that went
almost everywhere with him, he settled down to enjoy the
morning.

He was soon absorbed in his work. The woman who had written the diary was a good deal younger than her talented relative
and wrote of him with a certain flippancy, but nevertheless with
a great deal of respect. There were not really very many references to the famous microscopist. Mostly the writer had made
notes of her amorous adventures. Andrew read the crabbed
writing of the seventeenth century without much difficulty, for
by now he had had a good deal of practice in doing this. Now
and then he jotted down notes of what was relevant to his subject, and he had been busy with this for some time before he
became aware of two voices in the alcove next to him.

He did not pay much attention to them at first. They were
quiet and did not disturb him. One of the voices seemed somehow familiar, but he did not trouble to identify it. It was only
when one of them, not the one that he half-recognised but the
other, was suddenly raised with a sharp note of excitement in it,
that he found himself listening to what was being said. The
voice that had been muffled and indistinct for a moment was
distractingly clear.

It said, "Remember, all the same, I've got the knife."

Then there was hurried movement in the next-door alcove, a
chair scraped on the floor as someone presumably pushed it
back from the table there, got to his feet, and left.

Andrew rubbed a hand across his forehead, wondering if he
had actually heard what he thought he had, and if so, what it
meant. But in a moment he had forgotten about it and was once
more deep in the diary in which he had been so contentedly
absorbed.

It was only a few minutes later, however, that Gregory Ramsden appeared with a pleasant smile on his sharp-featured face

that gave it more expression than Andrew had noticed on it
before. He told Andrew that his wife was delighted that he
could dine with them, said he hoped that Andrew had had a
rewarding morning, arranged to pick him up at the staff club at
seven o'clock that evening, and then walked briskly away. Andrew looked at his watch and saw with some surprise that it was
a quarter to one. The morning had passed very quickly. Putting
his notebook into his briefcase and taking the precious diary to
the girl who sat at the counter in the hall, he made his way to
the staff club to have lunch there.

He spent the afternoon at a lecture on the metabolism of her-
bicides. After it he had a drink with a man who called out to
him by his Christian name, but who he did not recognize. But
the man reminded him that they had once been students together in the same London University department at least fifty
years ago, and as recollection trickled back Andrew found it
extraordinarily pleasant to remember and be remembered by
this old man who had had a career not unlike his own. They
spent about an hour together, then Andrew made his way to the
doorway of the club and stood there waiting until Gregory
Ramsden, in a grey Vauxhall of some antiquity, arrived to pick
him up.

The Ramsdens lived in a suburb of Knotlington about ten
minutes drive from the club. The street in which they lived was
a wide one of what had once been substantial brick-built Victorian houses, most of which, however, had been converted into
flats. The Ramsdens' flat was on the ground floor and when they
reached it Gregory Ramsden tooted his horn, which Andrew
took to be a signal, for almost at once the front door was opened
and a young girl appeared in the doorway, waiting there for
them to come in.

"This is my daughter Caroline," Ramsden said. "Caroline,
this is Professor Basnett."

The girl held out a hand to Andrew and said, "How do you
do, Professor Basnett?"

She looked only about nineteen years old, but she had an air of grave dignity, a look of calm self-assurance. She was slim and not very tall, with an oval face and neat, sharp features, dark hair that she wore rather long, falling in soft coils on her shoulders, and big, gentle brown eyes. She wore a flowered silk blouse and a straight, narrow black skirt, pearl earrings, and black flat-heeled sandals. Her neatness and trimness were altogether very like her father's.

"My mother's looking forward very much to meeting you after all this time," she said to Andrew. "She's sure you won't remember her, but she took her degree here in Knotlington and she's always said if it hadn't been for the help you gave her, coaching her, she'd never have made it."

Andrew found, when they met, that he had no memory whatever of Mrs. Ramsden. But this was not all his fault, for in one way at least she must have changed very much from the young woman she would have been when she attended his classes. Coming to meet him across a high, spacious room, she walked towards him leaning on two sticks, dragging both her feet slowly over the carpet. She had the bony angularity and the pallor of the invalid. When she smiled at him it seemed to be with an effort and her eyes had the deep-sunken look of someone in pain.

"It's so good of you to come," she said. "I know you won't remember me. You needn't pretend you do. In those days my name was Alison Gage. I wasn't one of your brighter students. But when Greg told me you were going to be here for this botanical conference I asked him to see if he could persuade you to come to dinner with us." Supporting herself on her sticks, she was leading him to a bay window where a tray with bottles and glasses was set out on a coffee table. "How does it feel, coming back to Knotlington? I've lived here most of my life and Greg's been here a good many years too, though he was in Oxford for some time before he came here. He used to think he'd like to see

if we could get back there, but then I had my accident and it
seemed sensible to stay where we were."

"An accident?" Andrew said. She had lowered herself carefully into one of the chairs by the bay window and had indicated
with one of her sticks that he should take a chair facing her. "A
car accident, was it?"

She nodded. "Yes, and it was all my own fault, looking the
wrong way and walking straight out into the traffic in a one-way
street. I was lucky not to be much more damaged that I was. I
was knocked unconscious, but the odd thing is I can still remember the scream the driver gave when she realised she couldn't
help hitting me. I've always felt bad about her. She was horrified
at what she saw was going to happen."

"It wasn't your fault at all," Gregory Ramsden said irritably,
as if this were a matter about which they had argued before.
"She was driving far too fast for a street like that. Even if you
did blunder out in front of her all of a sudden, she'd have had
plenty of time to pull up if she'd been going at a proper speed
and had been as sober as she should have been."

"All the same, I was lucky to escape without more damage
than I did," Alison Ramsden said. "I'd some trouble with my
spine and for a time I thought I wasn't going to be able to walk
again, but things haven't turned out too badly. What will you
have, Professor Basnett? Sherry, gin, whisky?"

Andrew chose whisky and Gregory Ramsden poured it out
for him. Andrew had sat down and was glancing about him.
There was an elaborate plaster cornice round the ceiling, a
heavy marble mantelpiece, bright cretonne-covered armchairs,
and light green wall-to-wall carpeting. There was a big bowl of
roses, carnations, and ferns in the empty grate, arranged with a
skill that made it look as if it had probably come from a florist.
But the first things that caught his eyes were two pictures on
either side of the fireplace. For a moment he was not sure why
they had caught his attention, then he recognised why of course
it was.

"Those are both Carl Judds you've got there, aren't they?" he said.

They were both of a yellow-haired woman who in one of them was busy peeling apples that apparently were going into a pie, and who in the other appeared to be entangled in the coils of a vacuum cleaner. Except for that bright yellow hair, which was held back from her face by a strand of black ribbon and which fell down her back almost to her waist, there were only dull, muddy colours in the pictures.

"How he liked to keep working hard," Andrew said. "Is that what she's really like?"

Ramsden laughed. "She's a charming, idle woman who enjoyed posing for poor Judd," he said. "Perhaps it was because she started life as an actress. Those two pictures are quite early works of his."

"Painted some time before his death, d'you mean?" Andrew asked.

"Oh yes, several years. As a matter of fact, I bought them at the first exhibition he had here. He was just beginning to make his mark. It was a pretty grim tragedy, you know, his death. Apart from the personal side of it, I believe if he'd lived he'd have turned out to be one of our major artists."

Andrew had only just noticed that Caroline, the Ramsdens' daughter, had not followed her parents to the bay window. He guessed that with a disabled mother it was probably the girl's job that evening to produce dinner for the four of them. He wondered what the girl did—whether running the household for her mother took up the whole of her time, or whether she had any independent occupation. Thinking about her, it struck him that she reminded him more of a girl whom he now vaguely remembered as having been called Alison Gage than she did of the crippled middle-aged woman sitting facing him across the coffee table. At first he had been so struck by Caroline's resemblance to her father that he had hardly noticed the deeper likeness to her mother. He felt that there was a great sadness in the fact that a girl who had the brisk, lively charm of her father should be held a captive, one might almost say, by her evident closeness to her mother.

"You know the story of the murder, I suppose?" Ramsden said.

"I've heard it," Andrew replied.

"To this day, you know, there are people who don't believe in Sharland's guilt."

"Then you do, I take it."

"No question of it."

Alison Ramsden sipped some sherry. "Try saying that to Margaret. The person who you'd think would be most certain of it won't hear of it. And when you listen to her, you begin to think she must be right. She's Carl's widow, you know," she explained to Andrew. "I believe what's at the bottom of it is that she can't face the fact that anyone could be guilty. Well, perhaps she's right."

"That no one's guilty?" Ramsden said. "Don't talk such nonsense."

"No, you know I didn't mean that," she said. "Only that perhaps it wasn't Sharland—it couldn't be someone they knew as well as they knew him."

"For God's sake, we've been over this so often and I'm tired of it," he said. "I think it might not be a bad idea to sell those pictures, then we might not find it cropping up so often." With a sound of firmly changing the subject, he went on, "How long are you staying in Knotlington, Professor?"

"Just till the end of the conference," Andrew answered.

"That's Friday, isn't it?"

"Yes."

"I hope it's been worth your while, coming here."

"Oh, it has."

The door opened and Caroline came in. She helped herself to a drink and joined the group at the bay window, sitting down on a sofa beside her mother.

"I hope you don't feel too ravenous," she said. "Things will be ready in about twenty minutes. It's only roast chicken and some ice cream from the grocer's. I'm sorry, Professor Basnett, I'm afraid I'm not a very good cook."

"She's a splendid cook," her mother said, giving her daughter's hand an affectionate pat. "What we'd do without her I can't imagine. I'm afraid she's allowed us to exploit her far too much. But at least she's managed to go on with what she wanted to do. She's been training in flower arrangement." She gestured at the bowl of flowers in the grate. "She's really gifted at it."

"Yes, indeed," Andrew agreed, though the girl made a gesture that indicated she did not enjoy talking of the subject. "Is there somewhere in Knotlington where you can really learn the job?"

"Oh yes," Caroline said, "and it's great luck for me because it's what I've always wanted to do. I suppose it's a thing one could teach oneself if one had to, but I'm working with Elfrida. She's my boss and she's quite well known. She's written a book about it. And she's a real artist and there's so much she's taught me. Some day, I suppose, I shall open a shop myself, and perhaps start giving classes, and . . ."

She broke off as the front door bell rang.

"That'll be Owen," she said, standing up.

"I didn't know you were expecting him," her mother said.

"I wasn't—exactly." A faint blush had coloured the girl's cheeks. She went quickly to the door.

As she went out Alison Ramsden smiled.

"Owen is someone whom we never exactly expect," she explained to Andrew, "but he has a way of turning up. A very nice boy, luckily."

The door opened again and Caroline re-entered, followed by a tall young man. He looked about twenty-five years old, was well built, dark-haired and dark-eyed and remarkably handsome in an aquiline, unusually distinguished way. He was wearing a well-cut grey suit with a white shirt and a blue tie, which made

Andrew feel sure, without thinking about it, that he had dressed carefully for some special occasion.

There was a look of excitement on Caroline's grave face. She forgot to introduce the young man to Andrew.

"Owen's been to London and he's got the job in Toronto," she exclaimed, thrusting her arm through his and leaning close to him. "It's all fixed up. He'll be going in a month's time, which gives us time to get married before he goes."

Her eyes were sparkling and she looked as if she hoped for exclamations of pleasure, perhaps for embraces and kisses.

What greeted her was silence.

# Three

IT SEEMED TO ANDREW that the silence lasted a long time, but when Alison Ramsden reached out a hand to the young man and drew him down to her and he kissed her cheek, Andrew realised that it had been only a moment.

It had been an uneasy sense of tension in the atmosphere that had made it seem longer. He thought he understood what had caused the tension. It came from a kind of fear in both Alison and Gregory. Their daughter was going to marry. She was going to leave them. Somehow her father and his crippled wife were going to have to learn how to organize their lives without any more help from her.

Andrew felt very sorry for them and also for the girl, though he was glad that she had not fallen into the trap of dutiful self-sacrifice. Perhaps it was a pity that she was about to go so far away from them as Canada. Or was it not? If a break had to be made might it not be best that it should be complete, and whatever solution her parents found for their sad problem, that they should not remain semi-dependent on her?

The job in Canada, Caroline explained to Andrew after she had remembered to introduce her fiancé to him as Owen Phillips, was with a firm of management consultants called Craig Deeping. Their headquarters were in Toronto, the pay was good, and there were prospects of promotion. And everything was wonderful and exciting and somehow a little incredible.

Still holding Owen by the hand, Alison smiled up at him and said, "I'm so glad you've made up your minds at last, my dears. And I hope you'll be very happy. Congratulations, both of you. Be good to her, Owen."

"You needn't be afraid that," he said with a quiet sound of pride in his voice. "I know how lucky I am."

"Well, now, I'd better see about that chicken," Caroline said. "Only shouldn't we have a drink first? I suppose it ought to be champagne, but actually I know Owen doesn't like it, so perhaps it's lucky we haven't got any in the house. We can start now as we mean to go on: He can have his own way as long as it doesn't stop me having mine. I think I'll have some sherry."

Owen had sherry too and Andrew and the Ramsdens had their glasses refilled and a toast was drunk; then Caroline darted off to the kitchen to dish up the chicken. Owen sat down and Gregory began to ask him questions about the job, about whether he thought that he and Caroline would make their home for good in Canada, and how soon they would actually be leaving. It seemed to Andrew that under the surface the tension was still there, but he admired the courage with which the Ramsdens set about concealing it.

The evening was a pleasant one, far pleasanter, Andrew thought, than he would have found the dinner of the Botanical Association. Formal dinners were events for which he had never much cared. If Caroline had told the truth when she said that she was not a good cook, if the chicken was on the tough side and if the ice cream that followed it had come from the grocer,

he felt the company more than made up for it. The kind of
happiness that shone in the eyes of the two young people was
something with which he had had no contact for a long time.
Since his retirement he had not seen much of the young, but
what he saw now evoked memories of when he himself had felt,
if only briefly, that nothing but love and delight and a joyous
wonder at the promise of life could lie before him.

Caroline brought coffee into the sitting-room, then retired to
the kitchen with Owen to do the washing up. Alison had only
just poured the coffee when the front door bell rang. Andrew
heard Caroline hurry to the door and talk for a minute or two to
someone in the hall; then she opened the sitting-room door and
a woman walked in. She came in leaving Caroline to go back to
the kitchen, as if this were something that she was used to doing. She had an air of belonging in the house, of having her own
position it it.

Alison exclaimed with pleasure, "Margaret!"

The woman answered, "Darlings! Caroline's just told me her
news. I don't believe she could have kept it in for a moment. I do
hope you're happy about it."

She looked about forty and was slimly and delicately built, of
medium height, with a narrow face in which her dark eyes
looked very big, and thick, long, bright yellow hair. It was
brushed straight back from her high forehead and tied in a
pony-tail with a strand of black ribbon. She was wearing black
corduroy jeans, a black and white striped silk shirt, and long jet
earrings, and she had several conspicuous rings on her long,
very slender hands.

Gregory Ramsden got quickly to his feet as she came into the
room, but Alison did not stir, except to lift her face so that the
other woman could kiss her cheek.

"Let me introduce Mrs. Judd, Andrew," Gregory said, and
turning to her, added, "Margaret, this is an old friend of Alison's, Professor Basnett."

"Professor Basnett," the woman echoed him thoughtfully, as

if the name meant more to her than Andrew could understand why it should. She held out one of her shapely hands to him and as he took it gave him a wondering, questioning look which he found puzzling.

He had not needed Gregory's introduction to tell him who she was. The yellow hair alone was enough to tell him that she was the woman whose portrait was on either side of the fireplace, busy in the one with peeling apples for a pie and in the other struggling to extricate herself from the coils of a vacuum cleaner. Yet the pictures were certainly not true portraits of her. Except for the mane of bright hair and something about the big dark eyes and the narrowness of the face, there had been no attempt to interpret her personality. In the pictures she was stocky, muscular, a woman accustomed to hard work. But the woman standing before him in the Ramsdens' sitting room had an ethereal sort of grace and lightness of which there was no trace in the paintings. It made Andrew wonder what had driven a man whose wife had such a fragile kind of beauty to endow her with the coarse and powerful characteristics of a peasant.

Her way of looking at Andrew made him feel as if she had believed that she had some knowledge of him which turned out to have been mistaken. It was not exactly that she looked disappointed so much as somehow bewildered. Apparently he was not what he ought to have been. But why she should have had any idea of what he should be he could not imagine.

Perhaps she realized that there was something in the way that she was regarding him that he found disconcerting, for with an abrupt movement she turned away and sat down in one of the armchairs, bringing her gaze back to Alison.

"But are you happy about it?" she asked. "Really happy?"

"Of course," Alison said.

"But how will you manage without Caroline?"

"Somehow," Alison said.

"Oh, I know when it comes to the point, you will. You always have. It's what you're like. But tell me the truth now, isn't it going to be difficult?"

"Perhaps, but we're glad it's settled at last," Gregory said. "They've been putting it off, you know, just on our account, and we haven't liked that. People don't stay young forever."

"What's tipped the balance now?" Margaret Judd asked.

"I think a talk Alison had with Caroline the other day," Gregory answered. "When that boy got the offer of the job in Toronto, which is just the kind of thing he's been wanting, she told Caroline how unfair on him it would be to stop him taking it because she wouldn't leave us. And at last Caroline told Owen that if he really wanted the job she was ready to go with him. And of course it's a little bit frightening for us, with Alison so helpless, but look how radiant they both are. It's what they've been longing for."

"And so it's worth it," Alison said.

"But how will you manage?" Margaret asked again. "I understand how you feel about it, but there are practical problems that will have to be faced."

"A home help might be all we'll need," Alison said. "But if the job's too much for her we can go to one of those agencies that supply someone who'll live in and do all the housekeeping and give me just the bit of help I'll need. And Greg will be retiring soon, so he can help. After all, it isn't as if there's any actual nursing to be done."

"Those women are awfully expensive," Margaret said.

"What isn't, these days?" Gregory asked. "Don't worry, we'll work something out."

"But listen to me, darlings," Margaret went on, "if you've any difficulty finding the kind of person you need, I mean if you haven't found anyone by the time Caroline wants to go away, remember I'm an idle woman and I could easily come in to help out till you're properly fixed up. Remember that, will you?"

"There!" Alison exclaimed. "That's just like her, isn't it, Greg?"

"But I mean it," Margaret said.

"Of course you do, and we'll remember it." Alison leant forward to pour out more coffee. "And we're very, very grateful."

"Only I know you and you won't make use of me, even though I really do mean it," Margaret said. "You might remember, perhaps, when you're thinking about such things, that I've a debt to pay."

"Now we won't talk about that," Alison said decisively. "There was never any question of a debt."

For a moment Andrew's eyes met Margaret Judd's, but she quickly looked away as if she felt that unintentionally, in that brief glance, she had betrayed something that she would sooner have kept hidden.

Andrew thought that he could guess what it was. It was something to do with help that the Ramsdens had given her at the time when her husband had been killed. Perhaps it had been no more than the kind of support that any friend might have given her, and it had happened to be by chance that the Ramsdens had been on the spot to do it, but to her it still meant far more than it ever had to them, and made her think of her relationship with them as something special.

But she did not want any talk of her husband's death that evening. It was a subject which at least for the moment was closed. Young love and happiness were in the air and were not to be darkened by tragedy.

It was about half past ten when Andrew began to consider how he should return to the hostel. The obvious way, it seemed to him, would be for him to telephone for a taxi since it was certainly too far to walk, but he was fairly sure that if he suggested doing such a thing Gregory would immediately insist on driving him back to the hostel himself.

There was no real reason why he should not do this except that Andrew felt reluctant to make use of him when it could so easily be avoided. However, the matter had to be settled some time, and as he had expected, as soon as he raised the subject of telephoning a taxi company, Gregory said that nothing would be easier than for him to drive Andrew to the hostel. But then Margaret Judd broke in, saying that the hostel was practically on her way home and that the sensible thing, of course, would be for her to take Andrew there. There seemed to be no point in arguing about this, and at about eleven o'clock she and Andrew said good-night to the Ramsdens and got into her car, which was in the road at their gate.

At first, as she drove, they talked of the days when Andrew and Nell had come to live in Knotlington. At that time Margaret Judd had been a schoolgirl, which seemed to amuse her. It was as if she felt that she had done something clever, growing up and closing the gap of years between them. Of course the gap, which was a little over thirty years, was the same now as it had been then. It was only that the long years of childhood had gradually shrunk to the far shorter ones of middle and old age.

When they had talked of this, having both confessed their ages, she gave him a quick sidelong look and said, smiling, "And if you don't mind my saying so, you've aged very well. If you wanted to claim you're ten years younger than you are, you could easily get away with it."

"In fact, if the subject comes up, I tend to do the opposite," Andrew said. "I'm inclined to add on five years or so to my actual age in the hope that someone will say how well preserved I am."

"Have you just done that with me?" she asked.

"No, I assure you I've trusted you with the truth. I'm seventy-two. Oh—!"

She started at his sudden exclamation.

"What is it?" she asked anxiously. "Oh, I see. Oh dear, I've been stupid." What she had done was drive straight past the gates of the hostel. "That's the sort of thing I'm always doing nowadays. Sheer absentmindedness." She had slowed down but had not stopped the car or shown any sign of being about to turn around. "What would you say to our going on a little far-

ther and your coming in with me for some more coffee? If you
could face it, I'd so much like to talk to you about some things
that are on my mind. I've felt it all the evening—I mean, that
you're the right person for me to talk to."

Andrew could not have said that he had expected this, but yet
in some way it did not surprise him. From the time that she had
entered the Ramsdens' sitting room, and had given him her first
strange, questioning look, he had sensed that sooner or later she
was going to want something of him.

"If it isn't too late for you then," he said, "I'd be delighted to
come in."

"Good." She accelerated again and in a few minutes turned in
at the open gateway of a house in a Georgian terrace in a wide,
quiet street. A quiet-looking house of grey stone with no lights
in any of the windows. A sober, well-proportioned, dignified
house. A house in which murder had been done.

She left the car in the small, paved drive-in before the front
door, and fumbling in her handbag for her keys, extracted them
from amongst a collection of papers, note-books, a note-case, a
purse, and what looked like a variety of cosmetics, and unlocked
the door. That handbag, bulging and untidy, was the first thing
about Margaret Judd that struck Andrew as out of character.
There was something so carefully elegant about her general appearance that he would have expected everything about her to
be neat and well organized.

She had only to switch on the light in the hall, however, and
take him into a small room to the left of the door for him to
realize that with the exception of her own dress and faint, clever
make-up, she was not in the least a well-organized person. The
room, which had one fine, tall window and an Adam-style fireplace, was a muddle of too much furniture of too many periods,
books lying on the floor, a sewing-machine on a table in front of
the window, heavy, faded curtains of crimson velvet, and one
enormous picture that covered nearly all of one wall, a picture
something like the one in the staff club which he had deduced

was a landscape because there were trees in it, but which also had a mysterious collection of wheels and human faces in the foreground.

Margaret went to the window and drew the curtains. Andrew liked her for making no apology for the untidiness of the room. It was a quite comfortable sort of untidiness and evidently was a part of her character, telling him at a glance far more about her than impeccable neatness would have done. She waved him to a chair and said that she would fetch brandy. The coffee appeared to have been forgotten. When she returned to the room after a few minutes' absence she had a tray with a bottle on it and two finely cut glasses which he thought were Waterford.

Putting the tray down on a coffee-table, she dropped down on the floor beside it, sitting cross-legged on a worn but still handsome rug.

"I'm going straight to the point," she said as she poured brandy into the two glasses. "You're Professor Basnett who knows all about murder."

Andrew, who had been leaning back comfortably in his chair with his long legs stretched out before him and his ankles crossed, jerked sharply upright.

"No!" he said harshly, almost fiercely. "Certainly not!"

She gave him a dismayed look, her forehead creasing into a puzzled frown.

"You aren't? You really aren't? You aren't Peter Dilly's uncle?"

Andrew relaxed with a sigh and leant back once more.

"Oh, so that's it. You know Peter."

"Then you are that Professor Basnett," she said swiftly. "I was sure you were, I didn't think there would be another."

"Peter's very imaginative, I'm afraid," Andrew answered, sipping his brandy. "I don't know what he's told you, but you'd probably be wise to cut it down by half."

"He's told me you've had some remarkable experiences, helping to solve murders. After my husband's death Peter said if ever I wanted advice about it, you were the person for me to go to. He said you're not only logical but very intuitive, and kind too. He said you'd help me. He's got a great admiration for you."

That at least, Andrew knew, was true. And the esteem was mutual. He and his nephew had not only always been the best of friends, but had a high regard for one another's very different talents. Peter had begun life as a schoolmaster, but after only a short time at that he had discovered a knack for writing very successful science fiction. As Andrew had said, he had a vivid imagination, and luckily for the young man it happened to be the kind of imagination that for some time now had been earning him an excellent income. He was very much richer than Andrew. But he was given to exaggeration and though Andrew had in fact once been involved with Peter in solving a murder, he suspected that Peter had probably given Margaret Judd an altogether too colourful description of what had happened then.

"Have you known Peter long?" he asked her.

"It was really my husband who knew him," she said. "They were at school together. They were very good friends there and later Peter used to visit us here occasionally. Then I met him accidentally in London about a month ago and we started talking about you. You know the story of my husband's death, don't you?"

He nodded. "I've heard a good deal about it since I got here."

"Well, Peter wanted me to go and see you, and I nearly did, but I hadn't the courage, and then the other day I heard by chance from Dr. Farmoor that you were coming here for the conference. And Greg Ramsden rang me up this afternoon to say that you were going to have dinner with him and Alison this evening, and suggested that if I still wanted to meet you I should come out to visit them. We've talked about you, you see, and he knew I'd wanted to meet you."

This at least cleared up something. If Margaret Judd knew Peter and had talked with him about what he had told her con-

cerning Andrew, with the Ramsdens, the little mystery of how
Gregory Ramsden knew of Andrew's interest in Robert Hooke
was explained.

"Was arranging that the debt you owed them that you talked
about?" Andrew asked.

"That? Oh no, that was—well, that was something more. It
was something they did for me when Carl was killed. But it's
part of what I wanted to talk to you about this evening. Only
when it comes to the point, I don't know where to begin. It's
complicated. And if you don't want me to do it at all, I won't.
We'll just have one brandy and I'll drive you back to the hostel. I
think perhaps by bringing you here I was taking rather a lot for
granted."

Andrew was not sure if he wanted her to go on or not. He was
tired. He was not at all happy about her apparent belief that he
was a skilled detective. He did not really like thinking and talking about murder. On the other hand, she had said enough to
rouse his curiosity as well as the beginnings of sympathy.

"If you really think I can help you," he said, "I'll be glad to
try. But I'm afraid you'll be disappointed."

She rubbed a knuckle against her forehead, as if she were
trying to obliterate the lines that had stayed there.

"Do you know about the portrait of Veronica Greenslade being slashed with the same knife that had been used to kill Carl?"
she asked.

"Yes," he said.

"Well, that's why I believe they arrested the wrong man, because Stephen Sharland would never have done that. He might
have murdered Carl in a fit of rage. I don't believe he would, but
I can just imagine it. Carl could be absolutely maddening. But
Stephen would never have slashed a portrait of Veronica."

Andrew waited for her to add something more to what she
had said, as it seemed to him a very incomplete statement, but
she seemed to feel that there was no need to do so. She only

looked at him in silence with a curiously challenging expression on her face.

"Why are you so sure he wouldn't have done that?" he asked.

"Because he'd no reason to do it," she said.

"He wasn't in love with her? He wasn't jealous? He didn't hate her? She hadn't harmed him in some way? She meant nothing to him?"

"The poor woman had committed suicide. That's absolutely all she'd done."

"It is, of course, a good deal to have done."

"Oh, yes, but it wasn't on Stephen's account."

"And the slashing of the picture is your whole reason for thinking Sharland isn't guilty of your husband's murder?"

She gave a deep and desperate sigh. "I suppose so, yes. And that's the trouble. It's such a small thing, isn't it? I tried to explain it to the police and the result of that was that they thought I must have killed Carl and slashed the portrait myself out of jealousy. Of course, if I had, the last thing I'd have done would have been to try to clear Stephen of suspicion, but still they seemed sure there was something peculiar about my doing that. And that's where the Ramsdens came in. That debt I mentioned. A lot of people thought I'd killed Carl. Most people, I think. And I was going nearly out of my mind, losing Carl and being frightened for myself, and being sure an innocent man had been arrested. And Greg Ramsden came round here and collected me and took me home to stay with them. I stayed with them for weeks, in fact until after the trial was over. And that just about saved my sanity."

"You know he and Mrs. Ramsden are sure Sharland's guilty?" Andrew said.

"Yes, and they know I don't think so. We're quite open about it. And so we can argue about it without me seeing that queer look come onto their faces that I used to see on other people's when they thought I was the obvious person to have slashed the portrait. Veronica and Carl did have an affair, you know, an affair of sorts. I never bothered to try to find out how far it went. Knowing Veronica, I should say not very far. But if you were married to Carl, you had to take him as he was."

Though she had not said so, and perhaps was not even aware of it herself, it seemed to Andrew that her debt to the Ramsdens was on account of their certainty that Stephen Sharland was guilty. Whatever her own belief about him might be, their conviction that he was guilty gave her reassurance that she evidently needed even after all the time that had passed since the murder.

"But exactly what is it you want to me to do?" he asked. "What *can* I do?"

"Couldn't you—? Oh, I haven't really thought it out, but couldn't you—well, investigate things? Ask some questions. Bring a fresh viewpoint to the matter. I thought you'd know yourself what you might be able to do, having had experience as Peter told me of solving a murder. You could open the whole thing up again, which I can hardly do myself. You know quite a number of the people here, don't you? If you started asking them questions they'd think it was just natural curiosity, and they might talk to you in a way they never would to me."

"But surely they've already told all they know to the police."

"Perhaps they haven't."

"Is that what you believe?"

"I think it's possible, anyway."

"And you really think I could get some information out of at least someone here which a trained detective didn't manage to dig up?"

"I think that's possible too."

He gave a shake of his head. "Don't you understand, my dear, I've no authority in the matter? I've no right to go round asking questions. Putting on a show of being just a nosy busybody is an act I might be able to keep up for a while, but it would soon begin to look suspicious. Believe me, I'd help you if I could, but I honestly don't see what use I can possibly be."

"You could try, couldn't you?"

"Where do you suggest I begin?"

She did not seem to notice the hint of irony in his tone.

"You might talk to Gwen Sharland," she said. "I've tried to do that myself, but she hates me so because she thinks I'm responsible for having Stephen convicted, she won't even speak to me."

Andrew thought of the woman of whom he had had a glimpse in the lounge of the staff club, the woman with the strange green eyes that so nearly matched the jade brooch she was wearing. He thought of the formidable air of purpose with which she had come and gone while he had sat talking with Giles Farmoor and stout little Kenneth Marriott.

"I don't know her," he said. "I've never exchanged a single word with her."

"I think we could arrange that," Margaret said.

He began to find her tenacity a little frightening, mixed up as it oddly was with what he thought was a kind of diffidence. To overcome that difference and stick to her determination to use him must take a good deal of courage.

"Suppose I say I'll think about it," he said. "I don't promise anything, but I won't say it's impossible to do what you want."

Her face brightened immediately and some of the tension went out of her slim body, still crouching on the floor. Till she relaxed she had not realized how tense she had been.

"I know you can't promise anything," she said, "but at least if you're going to try . . . I told you, Peter said you were kind."

"Well, perhaps we'd better begin here and now," he said. "Whom do you suspect?"

"Why, no one in particular," she answered, looking surprised at his question.

He did not believe her. "But isn't that the real reason why you're sure Sharland's innocent? You believe you know who the murderer was, and it's as important to you that that person shouldn't go unpunished as that an innocent man should be freed."

She shook her head so vigorously that her yellow hair swung
from side to side.

"No, I don't suspect anyone," she exclaimed. "I can't give you
any hints about where I think you should begin. At one time I
did wonder if it could be Professor Greenslade—because of Veronica, you know. If he thought she killed herself because of the
way Carl had treated her, he might have killed Carl out of revenge. It's the only motive I've been able to think of. But Carl
had plenty of other enemies. I think he liked having enemies
better than friends. But some of them, I daresay, were a good
deal crazier than Professor Greenslade. He's not at all a crazy,
violent sort of man under that quiet manner of his, would you
say?"

So after all Andrew had been given his hint, though he found
it difficult to take it seriously. However, it seemed to him the
most that he would get from her. He stood up.

"I think I'd better be on my way home," he said, "and I'll
think things over. Really, I'll see if I can think of anything useful I can do. But don't expect anything. I don't expect anything
myself."

By the next morning he was even more sure than he had been
the evening before, while he had been talking to the eager, im-
portunate woman, that there was nothing whatever that he
could do to help free Stephen Sharland, or alternatively to con-
firm that he was guilty. He felt a fool for having let himself be
talked into promising as much as he had, and thought that the
only thing to be done about the promise he had made was to
forget it. Also it might be wise to take what care he could to
avoid seeing any more of Margaret Judd. That should not be
difficult unless she actually came pursuing him. After she had
driven him back to the hostel and he had got out of the car she
said something about seeing him again soon, but no question of
any appointment had been raised and Andrew had begun to feel
as soon as she had driven away that she did not really expect

anything of him. She had been acting out some private drama of her own, in which she had no more belief than he had.

He went to bed as soon as he got back to his room and next morning overslept. It meant he had to hurry getting dressed, eating his little triangle of cheese, going to the refectory for breakfast, and then setting off for the lecture-theatre where a small symposium on the structure of the cell wall, which he particularly wanted to ~~wanted to~~ listen to, was to be held. As he  left the gardens of the hostel he was lucky enough to be offered a lift by some acquaintances and so arrived at the lecture-theatre early. At the entrance he came face to face with Walter Green-slade.

Seeing him now it seemed more fantastic than ever that the evening before he should have been seriously, or at least half-seriously, discussing the possibility that Walter was a murderer. His rather long, bland, smooth face had its usual expression of slightly smug calm. If the grey eyes behind his metal-rimmed spectacles looked more sunken and his colour more sallow than in the days when Andrew had seen him last, it seemed clear to him that it was a doctor who should make some inquiries into Walter's condition, rather than a detective. Distress on account of his sister's death, or the everyday worries concerning the running of his department, or perhaps mere overwork, could all account for the haggardness which gave him a look of unfamiliar strain, less absurdly than the suggestion that it might have been caused by deep and horrifying guilt.

Seeing Andrew, Walter grasped him by the arm, as his custom was, and drew him aside from the crowd that were thrusting their way in at the entrance to the theatre.

"What happened to you last night?" Walter asked. "We thought you were coming to the dinner?"

"I know," Andrew answered. "I'm sorry, I meant to come. But I got tied up with Ramsden and ended going to dinner with him and his wife. It didn't inconvenience you in any way, did it?"

"Oh, we didn't wait for you," Walter said. "But I was worried. I wondered if you'd had an accident or been taken ill or something."

"I'm sorry," Andrew repeated. "It was nothing like that. It was just that I got talking to Ramsden in the library and he asked me to dinner and I had one of my attacks of absent-mindedness and accepted before I'd remembered about the other dinner. Then by the time I did remember I thought he'd probably have phoned his wife to expect me, and that suddenly putting it off might put them out more than my simply not appearing at your dinner."

"Well, so long as that's all it was. By the way, have you seen Marriott this morning?"

"No."

"I'd an appointment with him in the department at nine o'clock and he didn't turn up." Walter sounded aggrieved, as if he felt that there was a conspiracy afoot to upset all the plans which it was his habit to make very carefully in advance. "He didn't even telephone to let me know he couldn't come. Not that it was about anything important, but he might have let me know he couldn't make it. If there's a thing that irritates me, it's when people don't keep appointments."

Andrew felt that this was meant at least partly for him.

"I ought to have tried to let you know I wouldn't be getting to the dinner," he said, "but I didn't know where to find you."

"Never mind, never mind," Walter said impatiently. "It didn't really matter. But I'm annoyed with Marriott. He could at least have got his secretary to let mine know that something had come up that stopped him coming to see me. He's a self-important little ass who thinks it's below him to concern himself with other people's convenience. What did you make of the Ramsdens?"

"Very charming people."

"I suppose so, yes." It did not sound as if Walter altogether agreed with him, though he added, "Great tragedy, that poor

woman's accident. Lucky for them they've got that daughter. It
isn't every girl of her age who'd stay at home to look after her
mother."

"Only she's leaving to get married," Andrew said. "You
hadn't heard about that?"

"No. Well, that'll be hard on them, but it's only to be expected."

"Mrs. Judd was there and she offered to help them."

"Margaret Judd?" Walter sounded startled. "She won't do it,
of course, for more than a day or two at the most. She's quite
irresponsible. Well, let's go in. I'd a vague hope Marriott might
think of looking for me here, but it's obvious that hasn't occurred to him."

Why it happened just then Andrew could not have said, but
something that had been puzzling him ever since he had met
Walter that morning seemed suddenly to become perfectly clear.
Yet really, even now, he was not entirely sure of it. For all he
knew, it could be something that was mostly fantasy. All the
same, for the moment he was quite certain of it, and it was only
when he began to think it over that doubt crept in.

Keeping close to Walter and listening to him carefully, Andrew thought with all the concentration that he could muster of
what Walter was saying. Andrew's problem was simply that it
had suddenly come to him that when he had been in the library
the morning before and had heard two people talking in low
voices in the alcove next to the one that he was occupying, one
of the voices had seemed familiar. He had not been interested
enough to listen and find out to whom it belonged. He had
simply forgotten about it. That was to say, he had let it stay
stowed away at the back of his mind, for now he could remember the voice quite clearly and it was Walter's.

Somehow talking of the Ramsdens and Margaret Judd had
brought it to the surface, perhaps because something that the
people in the next-door alcove had talked about had been a
knife. Not Walter's, but a voice that Andrew could not identify,

had suddenly spoken excitedly about a knife. A knife, could it possibly be, which had been used to stab a man and slash a portrait?

The morning seemed to Andrew to pass slowly. Although this was an event in the conference to which he had looked forward, he found it very difficult to pay attention to what was being said. He thought that Walter was in the same state of mind, though perhaps for different reasons. He kept his eyes shut a good deal of the time and when he opened them he only gazed absently up at the ceiling and when the time for lunch came round he muttered a hurried farewell to Andrew, got up and went quickly out.

Andrew did not hurry after him, but made his way out slowly with the rest of the crowd in the hall into the warm summer morning. He was joined by a few people he knew and together they walked towards the staff club, hoping that the crowd at the bar would not be too dense to make it possible to enjoy a drink.

It was fairly dense, but one of his companions took it on himself to obtain drinks for the rest of them and bring them to one of the tables at the other end of the lounge, if Andrew and the others in the group would keep the table for themselves. They were sitting there, waiting for the drinks to arrive, when Giles Farmoor came in.

At first Andrew thought that Giles had not seen him. He walked past the table, straight to the bar, with the distant, self-absorbed look on his face of someone who does not want to have any attention paid to him. But it was evident after only a few minutes that he had seen Andrew, because with two glasses of whisky in his hand and a strangely intense look on his face he came up behind him, bent over him, and said in a low voice, "Have you a little time to spare, Andrew? If you'd come over there with me, there's something I want to tell you."

Andrew stood up, apologized to the others for leaving them, and went with Giles to one of the tall windows where a wide window-sill could be made to act as a kind of table on which they could put their glasses, even though there was nowhere to sit down.

"What's wrong?" Andrew asked, because besides its tense expression, Giles's face, which usually had a healthy, freckled tan, had an unwholesome pallor.

"It's unbelievable," Giles answered, still in a half-whisper. "Marriott—Ken Marriott—you remember him?"

"Yes, of course," Andrew said. "We met in here the other evening."

"Yes, so we did. Well, being in the forensic department, you see, I was called in when they found him. Found him dead this morning, I mean. Strangulation. Murder. I'd like you to come along with me now and meet our Detective Superintendent Barrymore."

# Four

EVEN TO WALTER GREENSLADE, that most punctilious of men, Andrew thought, having been murdered must be an adequate excuse for failing to keep an appointment.

He realised that there was a certain absurdity about this being the first thing that he thought of after Giles had told him of Kenneth Marriott's death, but no one has complete control of his thoughts. It might be absurd, nevertheless that was how Andrew's mind worked at the moment.

He thrust his hands through his hair and sighed and picked up his glass and put it down again without having drunk anything.

"You say he was strangled," he said. "Was that done with some kind of cord or was it manual strangulation?"

"It was done with a length of nylon washing line. But first he was hit on the head with a bottle, to knock him out. That made the strangling easy." Giles swallowed his drink at a gulp.

"There was no sign of a struggle, and that nylon cord makes it look as if whoever did it came prepared to do murder. And it happened around eleven o'clock, or perhaps a little earlier, so they say. Now what about coming along to meet Barrymore?"

Andrew fingered his glass, but still did not drink from it.

"Giles, what would be the point of it? I'm not a detective. He'll only think I'm a nuisance."

"It might be a help to me. We could talk it over."

"We could do that without my having to meet the man. It's different for you. You belong here."

"But you've some knowledge of murder. You've solved more than one."

"That may not make me particularly popular with him. The professional, rightly, doesn't care much for the amateur. And you could tell me all that you find out and we could discuss it without my having to meet the man. I'll help you if I can, but I don't believe your Detective Superintendent will welcome having me under his feet."

"I want another drink," Giles said. "Wait a minute. I'll be back."

He picked up his glass and hurried towards the bar.

After two or three minutes he returned with his glass refilled.

"I'm feeling sick," he said. "I've seen a fair amount of murder, but not of people I knew quite as well as I knew Marriott. His face was blue and his tongue was sticking out and his eyes looked as if they might be going to fall out of his head. I never liked him, you know, but there it was, I knew him. The dead you know and the dead you don't belong in different categories. What do you want me to tell you about him?"

"The question is, it seems to me, what do you want to tell me?" Andrew said. "About the motive, for instance. Have the police any ideas about that?"

"Oh yes, plenty of ideas, only I don't really believe in any of them. We're supposed to assume it was burglary. Drawers had been pulled out and emptied onto the floor. Marriott's wallet was lying on the floor beside him and had been emptied. The kitchen window had been broken so that the latch of the back door could be reached and the door opened. Andrew, why not come along with me and meet Barrymore? He's a decent chap. You'll get on with each other."

A deep reluctance to become more involved in the affair than he could help kept Andrew silent for a moment. But then the fact that Giles was an old friend and that after all it was difficult to pretend to him, when of course he knew a good deal of Andrew's past that though as an amateur he had not had some experience of murder, made him feel himself beginning to yield to the pressure that Giles was exerting. But he resisted it still for a little while.

"Why shouldn't it have been burglary?" he asked. "It sounds convincing to me."

"Oh, it is," Giles said. "It's very convincing. Barrymore believes it. It's just my feeling that we've had a murder too many in this university. But of course Marriott's murder may have nothing to do with Judd's. Very likely it hasn't. But somehow I can't help connecting the two, though I can't see what the connection is. And if burglary wasn't the motive for killing Marriott, God knows what it was."

"D'you know, Giles, I've a very peculiar idea in my head," Andrew said, speaking slowly and thoughtfully. "It's because of something that happened yesterday. I was working in the library on a diary that I was interested in, and I was in an alcove by myself and getting along very pleasantly, and then it suddenly occurred to me that there were a couple of people in the alcove next to mine who were talking in low voices. But one of the voices was somehow familiar, though I didn't think much about it at the time, and it was only this morning I suddenly realised, while I was talking to him, that it was Walter's. And the other voice suddenly got excited and said fairly loudly that Walter was to remember he'd got the knife. I don't know what it meant, but you see, now that you're talking about him, I'm fairly sure that that second voice was Marriott's."

Giles's eyes for a moment opened wider and he gazed at Andrew with a look that was blankly incredulous. Whatever he made of what Andrew had just told him, it seemed he was not inclined to believe it. But then he returned to his demand that Andrew should go with him to meet Detective Superintendent Barrymore.

This time Andrew yielded, but insisted that first he wanted some lunch. He and Giles finished their drinks, then went into the restaurant and had a hasty lunch, after which Giles drove Andrew to the house, not far from Margaret Judd's, where Kenneth Marriott had met his end.

Like hers, it was in a Georgian terrace in a wide, quiet street. There were several police cars in the street, but when Giles took Andrew into the house it appeared that the ambulance which had been summoned to collect the body of Kenneth Marriott had already come and gone, taking away its silent passenger. Andrew was not sorry that he did not have to renew his acquaintance with the plump little registrar after strangulation had had its way with him.

Detective Superintendent Barrymore turned out to be a tall man, heavily built, with a thick neck, large projecting ears, not much hair left on his head, a blunt nose and small, shrewd grey eyes. He and a number of other men were wandering from room to room in the house, which was little more than a cottage. The body, Andrew gathered, had been found by Marriott's daily woman in the small sitting room on the ground floor. The house had two storeys as well as a basement, and it was through one of the basement windows, which opened into the kitchen, that the burglar, if in fact it had been a burglar, was thought to have got into the house.

The sitting room, from which the body had been removed, reminded Andrew in its proportions of the room in which he had sat with Margaret Judd the evening before, but it was sparsely furnished, with light-coloured modern furniture, and if the drawers had not been pulled out of a desk and emptied onto the floor, and if a cupboard had not been broken open and bottles and glasses swept out of it onto the carpet, and if the papers on a table had not been brushed off it and scattered carelessly around, it would have been a trim though rather characterless little room. But it looked as if there was very little in it to tempt a burglar, least of all a burglar determined enough to do murder.

Giles introduced Andrew to Superintendent Barrymore and induced him to tell the story of what he had heard in the library. Andrew did not think that the man was much impressed. However, he murmured, "A knife, Carl Judd was killed with a knife and the knife disappeared and has never been found. That makes your story interesting, naturally. Yes, a knife . . . well, thank you, Professor. That knife may be in the house somewhere. We must hunt for it, though of course it may be what our supposed burglar was looking for. I'll think about it."

"You don't believe then that all this—" Andrew gestured at the scattered papers and overturned bottles and glasses, "was just a common or garden burglary?"

"Oh, it may have been. Probably was. Much more likely than that it was something subtle and mysterious. All the same, we'll look for the knife. Only the trouble is that if it was what the murderer was looking for, he probably found it and took it away with him. He had all night to search. Thank you, all the same. Very interesting, what you've told me."

It was not exactly a dismissal, but it had the sound in it that Superintendent Barrymore had a good many other things to think about besides what Andrew had told him and that he would not take it amiss if Andrew and Giles should happen to remember at that point that they had appointments elsewhere.

Giles told Andrew that he intended just then to head for the central police station, but asked Andrew if there was anywhere he would like to be dropped. Andrew was about to say that he would like to be put down at the Botany Department when,

looking at his watch, he realised that he would arrive there in
the middle of that afternoon's session, which would not be very
rewarding. Instead he asked if Giles would drop him at the entrance to the Botanic Garden. The afternoon was fine, and to
stroll about on the perfectly kept lawns and perhaps to sit for a
while on a bench in the truly beautiful rose garden that he remembered or beside the lily pool would be a far more agreeable
way of spending the rest of the afternoon than sitting over a cup
of weak tea in the lounge of the staff club.

Giles did as Andrew asked, then drove off while Andrew
walked into the garden. It was not very big and in general was
regarded by the inhabitants of Knotlington as an agreeable little
park rather than anything of botanical interest. Once upon a
time it had been called the Physic Garden and had been devoted
mainly to the growing of medicinal herbs, but that was more
than a century ago. Starting down a grassy path which he knew
would lead him to the rose garden, Andrew wandered slowly
along, enjoying the sunshine, the quiet, the occasional sight of a
young mother with a stumbling infant playing with a ball or
suddenly falling flat on its face and setting up an indignant wail
at being so maltreated by life, and now and then on a bench an
old man or woman sitting alone and half asleep.

Andrew found a bench in the rose garden and soon felt inclined to fall asleep himself. If it had not been for the memory of
his talk with Giles and the thought of Kenneth Marriott spending a whole night alone and cold and dead in his house, he might
have done so. But every time that he actually closed his eyes a
vision of disturbing clarity, of Marriott as Giles had described
him, his face blue, his tongue sticking out and his eyes bulging,
sprang up before them. He also heard very clearly the voice that
he had heard in the library, which might or might not have been
Marriott's, claiming that he was in possession of a knife.

A knife which might have been used to commit murder, or
might, it was best to remember, have been some entirely harm-

less kitchen utensil that had never done anything more lethal than slice up a cucumber.

That did not seem particularly probable, but all the same it was as well to bear the possibility of some such thing in mind. Knives had many uses. Committing murder was only one of them, actually one of the rarer. . . .

Andrew came to with a start. He had been right on the edge of sleep and if someone had not come walking rapidly towards his bench just then with the clicking noise made by high heels on paving, he probably would have sunk deeply into slumber. But the sound woke him and opening his eyes he saw a tall woman coming quickly along the path between the rose beds, giving him a casual glance as she passed him, then walking on. The glance was very brief, but there was something singular about it. The eyes that dwelt on his face for a moment were of a very unusual shade of green.

Giving a great yawn, Andrew stood up. She was some yards beyond him by now and his first impulse was to hurry after her, catch her up and say that he was most anxious to speak to her. But as his mind cleared he recognized that it was most unlikely that she would let him do so. She would certainly mistake his intentions. She might be frightened, might run away, might scream, any of which would be very embarrassing. Drawing a deep breath to steady himself, Andrew waited till she was still farther away from him, then started walking quietly after her, making sure that the distance between them did not diminish.

As he followed her towards the gate he saw no sign that she was aware of his presence. She did not look back over her shoulder. She did not start to walk faster. Outside the gate she crossed the street and turned into a crescent of houses, went up some steps that led to the entrance of one of these, took a key out of her handbag and unlocked the door. She had just closed it behind her when Andrew reached the bottom of the steps.

He stood there, looking up at the house for a minute or two, hesitating about what to do next. Should he simply make a note of the address, hoping that it would come in useful some time or other? Should he go up to the door and ring the bell? Should he simply go away and do nothing further about the matter?

The last was what he very nearly did. He had not given Margaret Judd a definite promise that he would try to talk to this woman.

He had actually turned away and walked a few steps back in the direction of the main road when he turned abruptly, ran up the steps and rang one of the row of bells by the door. The house had evidently been turned into flats at some time and there were six bells, each with a card beside it on the doorpost. The card with the name Sharland on it was at the bottom of the row.

A moment passed before the door was opened, then the woman Andrew had followed to the house opened it and stood in the small hallway, looking him up and down. There was a door on either side of the hall from one of which she must just have emerged, for it was open. Behind her a steep staircase rose up to what were presumably the doors of other flats. The walls had been painted a dull cream and there was a carpet of dark brown on the stairs. It only just avoided being squalid, yet it was clean and some hunting prints on the walls suggested an attempt on the part of the landlord to introduce a little colour.

The woman was almost as tall as Andrew and as he remembered from his glimpse of her in the staff club, had a gawky kind of grace. Her fair hair, cut short except for a soft swirl across her forehead, made her look younger than perhaps she was. As she looked at him a puzzled frown appeared on her face. Neither of them spoke for a moment.

Then she said, "I know you. We've met, haven't we? No, I don't think we have, I'm sorry, I can't remember. I feel sure we have, but I can't tell you where. It's the stupid sort of thing I'm always doing nowadays. I hope you'll forgive me."

"It's my fault," Andrew said. "We didn't actually meet, but I was in the staff club an evening or so ago when you came in and

I suppose you caught sight of me and you've remembered it for no special reason. I happen to remember you clearly. I believe you're Mrs. Sharland."

Without quite frowning, she managed to look displeased, as if she did not like being reminded of her nightly trip to the bar in the staff club.

"Yes," she said. "But who are you? Are you on the staff here?"

"No, I'm only here on a visit," Andrew said. "My name's Basnett. I was once a professor of Botany, but I retired from that some years ago. I came to the conference here, held by the Botanical Association."

She looked uncertain, as if she felt half-inclined to ask him to come in and at the same time could not think what he could want with her.

"It isn't my husband you wanted to see, is it?" she said. "Because, of course . . ." The sentence faded and she made a vague little gesture with one hand, as if that should somehow end it.

"No, it was you yourself I wanted to talk to for a few minutes," Andrew said, "if that isn't too much of an impertinence."

"It probably is," she said. "I can't think why any retired and no doubt distinguished Professor of Botany should want to talk to me unless it's an impertinence. But you'd better come in and explain yourself. Of course, even if you don't want to talk to my husband, it's him you want to talk about? I'll leave it to you to judge for yourself whether I'm likely to tell you anything you want to know about him, or turn you straight out. There's something you do want to know, I suppose?"

"I think it's rather the other way about," Andrew said. "I was to tell you something. And I think it's something it might be useful for you to know, and anyway, it won't hurt you if I do come in. I'm fairly harmless."

A faint twitch of her lips which was almost a smile was her response to this, and, standing aside, she made a gesture inviting him in. He stepped into the small hall, then followed her in through the door inside that she had left open.

She took him into a living room where there were book-lined
walls, an electric fire set into one wall with a gilt-framed mirror
above it, a bright rug on the floor, some comfortable chairs and a
little dining table with four dining chairs pulled up to it. Dropping into a chair, she gestured to Andrew that he should sit
down on one that faced her on the other side of the fireplace.

"Well?" she said.

He immediately became tonguetied. He could not think what
he was doing there or what good it would do either of them if he
tried to explain why he had come.

Hesitantly he said, "Of course you know Margaret Judd."

He thought that she was going to leap from her chair and turn
him out of the flat there and then. But after drawing a deep
breath, she relaxed.

"Yes," she said.

"I was with her yesterday evening," he said. "We met at the
Ramsdens and she offered to drive me back to the hostel where
I'm staying while the conference is on. Then she said there was
something special she wanted to talk to me about, and we went
back to her house and drank some brandy and talked. We talked
mainly about you. She wanted me to get in touch with you and
tell you that she's sure your husband's innocent of her husband's murder. And she seemed to think I could help in some
way to find out what really happened. I told her I was sure I
couldn't, but I promised I'd do what I could. And this afternoon
I was sitting in the rose garden when I saw you go by and
however crazy it may seem now, I followed you home and
thought I'd see if I could talk to you. And if you want me to
leave, I'll go at once."

"Why couldn't she talk to me herself?" Gwen Sharland asked.
There was ice in her voice.

"She said you hated her and would refuse to talk to her."

She closed her eyes for a moment as if she were withdrawing
into herself, shutting him out. Then she opened them and gave a
slight nod of her head.

"She's right, of course, I do hate her. I think she's evil, cruel, and dishonest. But if she had tried to talk to me I wouldn't have refused to answer. I should merely have told her what I believe to be the truth. That is that she killed her husband and slashed the portrait of poor Veronica Greenslade. And that's why she won't speak to me herself. She couldn't have borne having to answer that."

"Was Carl Judd in love with Veronica?" Andrew asked.

"I doubt it."

"Was she in love with him then?"

"That's more probable."

"And you really think Margaret Judd killed him because of it?"

She made a harsh sound that might possibly have been a laugh. Leaning back in her chair, she pushed a cushion behind her head.

"I don't know what I think except that Stephen's innocent."

"Because he wouldn't have slashed Veronica's portrait?"

"Because he's Stephen. Because he's someone I happen to know rather well. He couldn't commit a murder. I don't need any more proof than that."

"Who do you think did slash the portrait?"

"Margaret, of course."

"In that case, why is she trying to clear Stephen of having done it? Isn't it to her advantage to have him thought the person who did it?"

"Yes, of course. But it may be she's realised that sooner or later it's going to come out that he'd never have slashed the portrait. Whoever did it either hated Veronica or her relationship with Judd. But Veronica meant nothing to Stephen. I think he rather liked her, but he didn't love her or hate her. And so Margaret wants to get in ahead of other people that he's innocent. After all, isn't it a kind of proof of her own innocence that she should want to do that?"

"That's a bit too subtle for me," Andrew said.

"It isn't really," she said. "You know the only evidence against him was the blood on his pullover which they found in our flat, and a story about a quarrel he'd had with Judd about one of his pictures, and of course what that awful man Marriott had to say about seeing Stephen come out of the Judds' house round about the time the murder was committed. And a lot of people never believed in all that, but thought Margaret was probably guilty. So if she takes their side that Stephen's certainly innocent, isn't that the best defence for her?"

"Marriott," Andrew said thoughtfully. "It sounds as if you don't know what's happened to him."

She gave him a puzzled look. "To Marriott? No, has something happened to him?"

Her gaze, which till then had not been focussed on anything in particular, suddenly became sharply concentrated on his face.

"No," she repeated, going on rapidly, "what is it? What's happened?"

He did not answer at once and even more swiftly she said, "Something's wrong. What is it?"

Sadly he said, "It's Knotlington's second murder. It happened last night. Someone got into Marriott's house and killed him. It either was robbery, or was meant to look like it. Drawers were pulled out, cupboards were emptied, the money had been taken from his wallet and so on. Anyway, Marriott himself was killed."

She gazed at him silently for what felt like a long time, then sat upright in her chair. A vivid smile suddenly appeared on her face, though her cheeks had become very pale.

"And Stephen didn't do it, did he?" she said exultantly. "No one can say he did. So is Knotlington just crawling with murderers, or were they wrong the first time?"

With an almost wild gesture, she pressed both her fists against her mouth as if to hold in what might have come out as hysterical laughter.

"I suppose either is possible," Andrew said. "It's two years,

isn't it, since Judd was killed? And that's quite a long time. Time
for a new murderer to have appeared on the scene."

"How was Marriott killed?" she asked. Her voice had become
tense and shrill. "Was it the same way as Judd? Was he stabbed
with the same knife?"

"No."

"Oh." It was only natural, he supposed, that there should be
disappointment in her tone. "You're sure it wasn't?"

"According to what I've been told," Andrew said, "Marriott
was strangled."

"Who told you?"

"Dr. Farmoor."

Her look of disappointment deepened, as if something said by
Giles Farmoor had to be taken seriously.

"It doesn't make much sense, does it?" she said. "I mean that
this could have had anything to do with Judd's murder. Two
years, as you said, is a long time. No, for a moment I had a hope
. . . No. All the same, why don't you ask me for my alibi?"

"Do you need one?" Andrew asked.

"Well, I haven't one, you know." Her voice had become dry
and ironic. "If Marriott was killed sometime yesterday evening,
I've no alibi at all. I was at home here. I washed my hair. I wrote
some letters but I didn't go out to post them, so no one can have
seen me go to the letter-box. I watched the news on television.
. . . Oh God, what a fool I'm being! What I did or didn't do
doesn't amount to anything. And of course, as I'm sure you'll
tell me, it isn't your business, and you're much too courteous to
probe and pry. I'm insulting you by pretending that that's what
you want to do. All the same, I've a motive for killing that vile
little man, Marriott, haven't I? And has anyone else?"

"You don't believe in the burglar, then?" Andrew said.

"Do you?"

"I don't see why not. Of course, I don't know a great deal
about the people here, so I've no idea who may have had a motive for murdering Marriott. For all I know, it may be yourself

and you may need that alibi you say you haven't got. But suppose you tell me who besides yourself you think may have had a
convincing sort of motive. If the fact is that you've just taken
revenge on him for having had your husband convicted of
Judd's murder, you've waited a very long time to do anything
about it. So it seems to me that if you had anything to do with it,
it would have to be for some other reason."

She gave a bitter little smile, which was in some way frightening. Andrew recognised that there was a twist in her nature
which made it conceivable that she might be ready to wait even
two years before she took revenge for some real or imagined
wrong.

"If I troubled to do anything about Marriott, it would be for
one reason, and that was for what he did to Stephen," she said.
"I don't know who else may have hated him or feared him."

"Feared him?" Andrew said.

"Yes, there's someone around who may have been very afraid
of him. I mean the person who really murdered Judd. Someone
who knew that Marriott knew the truth about him."

"You're thinking of blackmail."

"Well, doesn't it seem to you as good a motive as any? It's
generally considered one of the best."

"Only it doesn't get us much further, does it, until we know
more about Judd's murder?"

But as he said it, Andrew had a strange feeling that he knew
more about Judd's murder than he had yet quite understood.
Some thought was stirring in his mind, struggling to reach the
surface. In some way it linked the two dead men, Carl Judd and
Kenneth Marriott. Though their deaths were two years apart,
something connected them with each other.

Andrew took his leave of Gwen Sharland only a few minutes
later, after apologizing for having intruded on her as he had. She
held his hand for a moment as he was saying good-bye, and
seemed on the edge of saying something which might have been
a suggestion that he should come to see her again when he had

more to tell her. But then she withdrew her hand abruptly as if it was he who had been holding hers too long. Andrew went down the steps into the crescent and set off for the main road.

He walked back to the staff club, which was a fair distance away, but the late afternoon had still a summery warmth and the walk was pleasant. The gardens of the houses that he passed were gay with flowers. The brightness of the sky had softened to the delicate pallor of coming evening.

As he walked, Andrew found himself once more muttering under his breath:

> *"There is a Reaper, whose name is Death,*
> *And with his sickle keen . . ."*

Quietly he interrupted himself to swear. It infuriated him to catch himself out reciting this undistinguished stuff. Longfellow, he had always thought, was a deplorable poet, and though his Reaper appeared to have been rather busy here in Knotlington just lately, there was no reason why a retired professor of Botany should go on reciting him pointlessly to himself on an agreeable walk on a fine afternoon through the quiet streets of this not unpleasant town. He strode on faster as if that would help him to escape from the verse that he so disliked.

The feeling that there was something about the murder of Carl Judd that he should have understood quite easily if he had been as awake as he ought to have been stayed with him as persistently as Longfellow, and after only a short time he realised what it was. But whether or not it really meant anything he was not sure at all. It went back to that morning he had spent in the library when he had been so deeply absorbed in the diary of Robert Hooke's relative that he had paid hardly any attention to the two voices he had heard quietly talking in the alcove next to his. But little as he had listened to them, he had become aware that one voice was probably Walter Greenslade's, and still later on it had come to him that the other voice, the one that he did

not know, or rather hardly knew, was Kenneth Marriott's. A
voice that had claimed with a sound of excited triumph that he
had 'the knife.'

But had the voice really been Marriott's?

Marriott was dead and it was impossible to check if that second voice had been his. But suppose that it had been. And suppose that the knife he had been talking about was the one that
had stabbed Carl Judd to death and then slashed the unfinished
portrait of Veronica Greenslade. And suppose that the person to
whom Marriott had been speaking had been Walter Greenslade.
Did that not add up to the probability that Marriott had been
telling Walter that he knew he was Judd's murderer?

Yes, if all those suppositions were correct, it meant that Walter was Judd's murderer.

Preposterous as that sounded, the truth was, it all fitted together rather well. Walter, after all, had had a tolerably good
motive for murdering Judd. Walter had been devoted to his sister Veronica and it seemed likely that she had been driven to
taking her own life by Judd's treatment of her. Then if Marriott
had somehow found this out and had taken possession of the
knife which had Walter's fingerprints on it and had threatened
him with blackmail, it gave Walter a motive for murdering Marriott. And the disorder in Marriott's house might not have been
intended to simulate burglary but had been simply the result of
a desperate hunt for the knife which Marriott had kept hidden
somewhere. Certainly it all fitted together very well.

But it meant accepting rather a lot of suppositions. And could
a man who had once been your student and whom you had
known for years be a murderer? Could you bring yourself to
believe that? And the evening before, when Marriott had been
killed, Walter had been at the dinner of the Botanical Association. That was a pretty good alibi.

And why should Marriott have waited two years to start his
blackmailing of Walter? Or if it had been going on for all that

time, why should the paying of it suddenly have become intolerable? There would have to be a reason for that. Something must
have happened recently to bring it about.

Yes, something must have happened.

# Five

LATER, IN THE EARLY EVENING, Giles Farmoor joined Andrew in the staff club and removed him from the group of old acquaintances who were happily discussing the mechanism of stomatal activity. They settled down in a corner of the lounge and Giles asked him how he had spent the afternoon since he and Andrew had parted after leaving Kenneth Marriott's house.

Andrew told him of his meeting with Gwen Sharland and of the talk that they had had in her flat, but nothing of the thoughts that had been pursuing him since he had left her concerning the possibility that Walter Greenslade, of all unlikely people, had been the murderer of Carl Judd.

Having had time to think it over, Andrew had decided that he did not believe in this for a moment. If he had not been so unfortunate at different times during the last few years as to become involved in the solution of a murder or two, so that he was more inclined than he would have been before he had been drawn into that rather gruesome activity to think that his own wild guesses were sometimes perhaps to be taken seriously, he would not even have considered such a possibility.

Certainly he did not want to discuss it with anyone else, even with Giles. He had a feeling that Giles had something that he wanted to confide in him, and if this were true Andrew was ready to hear what it was without having to prompt him. He found himself thinking of Gwen Sharland, finding that she had made more of an impression on him than he had realised at the time. Her tall, angular grace, her sardonic intelligence, her loyalty to the man in prison who, whatever she actually believed, was probably a murderer, had a bitter kind of interest. If Andrew had been many years younger than he was he might have been strongly attracted to her.

As he waited while Giles fetched drinks for them both, he found himself thinking of her, wondering if she would make one of her sudden intrusions into the bar and if she did whether he could persuade her to join him and Giles. Probably not. All the same, he would like to know her better.

She had not appeared when Giles brought their drinks to the table at which Andrew was waiting. Giles was looking tired and yet eager to talk, with an air of impatience about him, almost as if he found Andrew's passive calm, as he waited for him to talk about whatever was on his mind, somehow irritating. He wanted Andrew to be as eager as he was himself to discuss matters of life and death, of guilt and innocence.

"I'm sorry you and Barrymore didn't hit it off better than you did," Giles said. "I like him myself. I thought you'd get on better than you did."

"We got on all right," Andrew said. "It was just that he's a professional, and as I said to you before, like professionals in all walks of life, whether acting or painting or driving racing cars or solving mysteries, he's got a justified contempt for the amateur. I was entirely in sympathy with him. It was natural for him to expect that I'd just waste his time."

"You're very tolerant," Giles said. "If that's really his attitude he must miss a number of valuable leads."

"Very few, I imagine," Andrew said. "Take today. I hadn't much to tell him."

"Well, I heard something today which you may find interesting," Giles said. "When I was talking to Barrymore after he got back to the police station this afternoon, he told me something which may mean quite a lot. It's that Marriott almost never cashed a cheque. He had an account at the National Westminster, and his monthly salary cheques were paid straight into his current account there, but he almost never drew anything out, except to transfer it to his deposit account. Does that mean anything to you?"

"It suggests either that he'd another account in some other bank, which the police haven't come on yet," Andrew said, "or else that he'd some private source of income."

"Exactly," Giles agreed with a satisfied smile. "Income paid to him in cash. And what is that likely to mean?"

"That he was dodging income tax."

"Oh come, Andrew, you know better than that."

"You don't think he was dodging income tax?"

Giles laughed. "Look, I know you're doing it on purpose. Of course he was dodging income tax, but you know as well as I do that that isn't the whole of the story."

Andrew laughed too. He had, of course, been tempted into irritating Giles a little.

"Well, I suppose I do," he said. "All right then, he was being paid blackmail. Isn't that what you want me to say?"

Giles gave a solemn nod.

"Do the police know yet who was paying him?" Andrew asked.

"I don't think they're even convinced yet it was blackmail," Giles said. "That's just my own interpretation of the situation. They're still being very cautious. But if what you told me is correct, that Marriott told Greenslade in the library that he'd got some knife or other and it sounded as if he was threatening Greenslade, then isn't it more than probable that Marriott had some hold over him and was probably extorting a useful income from him?"

"In other words, that Walter murdered Judd and somehow Marriott found it out and got hold of the knife, which may have had Walter's fingerprints on it?" It shocked Andrew to hear himself say it.

"Why not?" Giles asked.

"But Greenslade didn't murder Marriott, did he?"

"Because he was at the dinner here about the time Marriott was killed?"

"Yes."

Giles leant back in his chair, looking up vacantly at the ceiling. After a moment he brought his gaze back to Andrew's face. He was frowning slightly.

"How sure are you, Andrew, that the one voice you heard in the library was Greenslade's and the other was Marriott's?" he asked.

"Not sure at all," Andrew replied cheerfully. He felt that by saying this he shed some of the responsibility for possibly incriminating two quite innocent men, and it made him feel more at ease with himself. "It could easily have been two quite different people."

Giles looked annoyed. "I don't think I believe you," he said.

"Honestly, it isn't a thing I'd dream of swearing to in court," Andrew said. "I do *think* it was Walter and Marriott talking to each other, and I agree with you that Marriott could have been blackmailing Walter. But if one swallows that, then of course one's got to swallow the fact that Walter murdered Judd, unless there was some other crime he'd committed for which Marriott was blackmailing him. Can you think of any other crime— fraud, bigamy, indecent assault—that Walter might have committed?" He could not keep the flippancy out of his voice.

"I wish I knew what you really think," Giles said discontentedly.

"So do I," Andrew answered. "It would make life much easier."

"What are you going to do about it?"

"*Do!*" Andrew said in a shocked voice, as if this was really going too far. "Why, nothing at all."

"You mean you intend to let Greenslade get away with having committed two murders?"

"Giles, I don't know for certain that he's committed *any* murders."

"All right," Giles said, "I know what you're like when you get into this mood. One can't get anything positive out of you. Now, suppose you come home to dinner with me. I'm getting tired of this place, and at the moment I don't feel inclined to get tied up in social chat with Greenslade, as we'd probably have to if we stay on. I don't know what there'll be to eat at home, but I don't think we'll starve. We'll probably find that my Mrs. Warburton, who runs my life for me, will have left a reasonably adequate meal behind, even though she wasn't expecting a guest."

Andrew, who found suddenly that he felt quite ready to escape from the club, thanked Giles for his invitation, finished his drink and set off with him to his home.

Giles lived in a flat in a tall modern block near the centre of the city. He was unmarried and had always lived alone except for short periods when he induced some woman to move in with him for a time. He liked women, liked some occasional sex and some companionship, but he was normally a solitary man, kind and generous in his way but needing seclusion more than he needed friendship.

Perhaps this tendency in him had been exaggerated by his work, which brought him continually into contact with those who had nothing to say to him, nothing to give him, and who could not respond to him in any way. The dead are not very

stimulating company and he spent all too much of his time
amongst them.

His flat was comfortable and moderately attractive in an im-
personal way. The furniture was Scandinavian, the walls were
white, the curtains and carpets were in the various shades of
brown that Andrew always associated with Giles, from his hair
*and* his freckles to his well-polished shoes, and if it had not been
for shelves of books that covered one wall of the small sitting-
room, it would have been distinctly colourless. The woman
whom Giles had referred to as his Mrs. Warburton, who came in
every morning after he had left for work to clean the flat and do
what she could to organize his life, had set a place for one on the
table under the window, with a note propped up against a wine-
glass to tell him that there was a steak and kidney pie in the
oven and what he ought to do about warming it up. Giles
checked that the pie was big enough for two, then set a second
place on the table, and poured out sherry for Andrew and himself to pass the time while they waited for the pie to be ready.

Sitting on either side of the electric fire, which naturally was
not switched on in this midsummer warmth, they went on talking of Marriott's death and of what it had brought to light.

"There's something I haven't told you," Giles said. "Barrymore mentioned it to me only just before I started out for the
club, hoping I'd find you there. I think he'd only just found it
out himself. It's a curious thing and I don't pretend to understand it. Ever since her husband's death Margaret Judd has been
drawing five hundred pounds every month out of her own bank
account. The cheques are all made out to self, but she also runs
accounts at several local shops which she pays regularly by
cheque, and if the five hundred is added on to these, it means her
personal expenses come rather high for someone who lives alone
in the sort of way she does. Of course it may mean nothing. She
may simply be a fairly extravagant person, or she may have
some aged relative she's supporting and she's pinching herself to
do it. I've no idea where her income comes from or how much

she's got. I don't know if she's getting a pension from the University, but even if she is, it can't be much."

"So we're talking about blackmail again, is that it?" Andrew said. "That's where you think the five hundred is going."

Giles made a wry grimace. "I admit I seem to find it difficult to keep off the subject for long," he said. "But suppose it's blackmail, doesn't it look as if it's being paid to someone who happens to know Margaret Judd had something to do with her husband's murder?"

"I spent some time with her yesterday evening," Andrew said. "Like you, she seems to be convinced Sharland's innocent, and this afternoon I was talking to Mrs. Sharland, and she's got a complicated theory that that's Mrs. Judd's way of making out she's innocent herself. Mrs. Sharland's convinced, so I understand, that Mrs. Judd killed Judd and slashed the portrait of Veronica out of jealousy. Of course, if that's correct, the five hundred a month may have been going to Mrs. Sharland—except that if she really had something on Mrs. Judd she'd have used it, one supposes, to get her husband out of prison, unless she's a much more devious person than she seems to be."

"How have you been getting in touch with all these women?" Giles asked, his crooked smile appearing again. "I wouldn't have expected you to be such a fast worker."

"I met Mrs. Judd at the Ramsdens'," Andrew said. "I had dinner with them last night, and Mrs. Judd dropped in, then offered to drive me home. But then it turned out that she wanted to drive me to/on her own home and have a talk about her husband's murder. She knows a nephew of mine, and she'd got it into her head from talking to him that I'm a great detective who'd help her to get at the truth about Judd's death. I did my best to disillusion her about my abilities, but I ended up saying that if I'd a chance to talk to Mrs. Sharland, I'd see if I could get anything out of her. I didn't really mean to do anything about it, but then by chance I ran into Mrs. Sharland this afternoon and found myself trying to get what information I

could out of her. A lot of time wasted. I can't help either of them
and I'm wishing I'd never had the bright idea of coming to
Knotlington to this conference."

"Poor Andrew, I'm sorry for you." Giles's tone was mildly
malicious. "What did you make of Margaret?"

Andrew had not yet asked himself what he had made of her.
He could have answered the question more easily if Giles had
asked him what he had made of Gwen Sharland. He was inclined to think that of the two women he liked Margaret Judd
the better, yet she had made less impression on him than the tall
woman whom he had followed to her home across the Botanic
Garden.

"If you're asking if she seems to me a likely person to have
murdered her husband," he said, "I suppose the answer is no.
But the murderers I've encountered myself in the past have
been very unlikely people, all in all."

"I wasn't thinking of that specifically," Giles said. "I'm more
interested really in the question of how she put up with Judd for
as long as she did. She always seemed to be devoted to him, and
if she was suddenly going to murder him out of jealousy she'd
have had plenty of reason to do it before Veronica came on the
scene. But perhaps jealousy's a disease you develop all of a sudden like flu, without knowing where you picked it up."

He went out to the kitchen and after a few minutes returned
with a splendid-looking pie, which was followed presently by
biscuits and cheese. He and Andrew sat down at the table, and
over their meal somehow succeeded in getting away from the
subjects of murder, of blackmail, of women whose actions might
be highly suspicious or quite innocent.

After that they watched the news on television and not long
after that Giles would have driven Andrew back to the hostel if
there had not come a ring at the doorbell.

Muttering something irritably, because he had no desire for
another visitor, Giles went to the door and upon opening it
found Detective Superintendent Barrymore on his doorstep.

Giles did his best to look pleased at this, invited the Superintendent in and supplied him with a whisky. Andrew, knowing Giles as well as he did, realised that by now he had reached the stage of looking forward to spending the rest of the evening quietly by himself, reading a favourite Trollope for a while before going early to bed. But Barrymore was not able to interpret the expression on Giles's friendly but unrevealing face as easily as Andrew was, and apparently did not dream that his visit might be unwelcome.

Settling himself comfortably with his drink in one of the chairs by the fireplace, the Superintendent observed, "I happened to be in the neighbourhood, Dr. Farmoor, so I thought I'd drop in. Not too late for you, I hope. We've just learnt something which I thought you and Professor Basnett might find interesting. We've had a visit from Mrs. Judd. No telephone call or anything beforehand. She just walked into the station and asked to see me. Then she told me she's been paying five hundred a month to Mrs. Sharland for almost two years to help her out as she's been left more or less penniless ever since her husband went to prison. And Mrs. Judd said she's been brooding about it, because if we stumbled on the fact by ourselves, she thought, and didn't know why she'd been doing it, it could look as if she'd been paying Mrs. Sharland blackmail. In other words, we might think the Sharland woman knows something about the Judd murder which would incriminate Mrs. Judd and we'd start making trouble for her. Apparently she's quite a well-to-do woman. Her father, who died about two years ago, was a successful surgeon who left her all he had when he died. A bit naive of her to think we'd swallow her story just like that, but it seemed she thought she'd only got to tell it to us to convince us."

"And of course it could be true," Giles said.

"Ah, but it isn't," Barrymore said.

"How d'you know?"

"Well, naturally, the first thing we did was get in touch with

Mrs. Sharland to hear her side of the story, and she said flatly
she'd never been paid anything by Mrs. Judd, that she isn't penniless but has a quite reasonable income also left her by a father,
as well as a job, and that if Mrs. Judd has been paying considerable sums of money to anybody ever since her husband's death,
it was probably to Marriott. And that probably it was blackmail
because he knew something about the Judd murder and Judd's
wife's part in it."

"Just a minute," Andrew said. "I've been over this before and
I'd like to know why, even suppose all the rest of it is true, and
Mrs. Judd was at least somehow involved in her husband's mur-
der, she waited two years to kill Marriott, or to get him killed.
Why didn't she do it right away? She must have had plenty of
opportunities."

"That's true," Barrymore said, nodding his head wisely.
"Thank you, Professor. It's a point I was just about to make
myself. And it seems to me to indicate that something significant has happened recently. Perhaps it's simply that Mrs. Judd
suddenly got tired of paying so much money to Marriott. Nothing rational, you know. Just a frantic feeling that she couldn't
stand it any longer. Or perhaps he tried to increase the bite and
went too far. Or perhaps she needed the money for something
else that's only just come up. There are all sorts of possibilities.
But for certain, something's happened recently that changed the
situation."

"That's for sure," Giles said. "If there's a word of truth in
what you've told us, something's happened."

So there they were, all at the very point at which Andrew had
arrived in the afternoon after his talk with Gwen Sharland
while he had been walking back to the club. Something of which
Barrymore knew nothing, nor Giles, nor anyone else about of
whom Andrew had heard since coming to Knotlington, had certainly happened.

When Giles presently drove him back to the hostel, Andrew
found himself restless and not in the least inclined to go to sleep.

He got into bed and resumed reading the Eric Ambler that he had started the evening before, but even by the time he got to the end of it he was still as wakeful as ever. He began to think that there was really no reason why he should not return home next day. From his point of view the conference, as such, was a failure. It had held next to no scientific interest for him. That, of course, was his own fault. The truth was, he was getting too old for this kind of thing. He was out of touch with all that would have interested him once and he could not avoid the feeling, when he found himself in a group of men much younger and more active than he was, that any deference they showed him came merely from courtesy and not from any regard for work that he had ever done. Most of them had never heard of him, just as, to tell the truth, he had never heard of them. His home began to seem a very attractive place. Time passed, and it was with a start that he woke up to realise, when he looked at his watch, that he had been asleep for several hours.

He had a shower, shaved and got dressed, ate his small but very important ration of cheese, then went downstairs to breakfast. When he had had it, he drifted indecisively to the university library and asked once more for the diary that he had been reading before with such interest.

It was brought to him, but today he found that he could not concentrate on it. He could not help listening for voices in the alcove next to the one in which he had settled down. But no voices came to him from it. It appeared to be unoccupied. Feeling that he was wasting his time, he got up and was on his way out of the library when, just before he went out into the street, he encountered Gregory Ramsden.

Ramsden suggested that he should come to his office with him for some coffee. Andrew hesitated. Once again the idea of returning to London seemed suddenly very attractive. But to refuse the invitation when he did not even know the time of the next train and when he should set off to catch it, seemed unpleasantly discourteous. He thanked Ramsden and went with him up a wide staircase and along a passage to a door on which appeared "Dr. G. Ramsden."

Ramsden's usual briskness seemed changed to a curious state of nervous excitement. When he had ordered coffee on his desk telephone, he began to walk up and down the room, appearing to have forgotten to invite Andrew to sit down

"Of course you know about poor Marriott, don't you?" he said and then, without waiting for Andrew to answer, went on: "But you don't know much about any of us here, do you? I know you've known Farmoor for some time, and of course Greenslade, but I don't suppose you know what to make of things in general."

Andrew decided to take a chair for himself.

"Do *you?*" he asked.

Ramsden gave him a puzzled glance, as if he did not understand the question and was not sure if he was meant to take it as something requiring an answer. Then he gave a short laugh, as if he had just seen a joke, and said, "Good Lord, I suppose not. No, of course not. I see what you mean."

Andrew doubted if he did see what he meant, since he was not even sure of it himself. But at least it brought Ramsden to a standstill, and after looking vaguely round the room, he dropped into the chair at the desk.

"The police came to see me this morning, you know," Ramsden said. "They've been round a good many of the people here, so I've heard, asking when we saw Marriott last, and whether he seemed normal when we saw him or worried about anything and that sort of thing. I said I'd understood he was probably murdered by someone who'd broken into his home, anyway that was what I'd been told by—let me see, who was it who told me that?—it was Allbright. I don't expect you know him. He's Marriott's assistant. And the detective who was questioning me said that that was what it was meant to look like, but that they'd got to explore every avenue and what they were checking up on was whether there was any indication that Marriott had been scared in any way before he was killed. Well, I told him I hadn't seen him since last week and that I certainly hadn't noticed any sign in him that he was expecting to be murdered, and the man got quite annoyed with me, as if he thought I was being flippant. But ask a silly question and you'll get a silly answer. I mean to say! As if the poor chap could have been *afraid* of getting murdered in a place like this! Who do they think run Knotlington University? The Mafia? I know the place has its faults and we may have a bad reputation because of Judd's murder, but that was a long time ago and the University Grants Committee has never supported us in keeping a department of homicide going. And this man and I got well and truly across one another. And then, when I thought I'd put him in his place and he'd cleared out, an awful thing suddenly struck me. I'd told the man a lie. Actually it wasn't last week that I saw Marriott last, it was the day before yesterday. It was here in the library. And I can't make up my mind what I ought to do about it. What do you think?"

"The day before yesterday," Andrew said thoughtfully. "So it *was* Marriott who was in here."

"Well, he was in here for a time, talking to Greenslade," Ramsden said. "You were in here yourself, in the alcove next to them. Greenslade told me he'd come in to check up on some references he wanted for a speech he'd got to give that evening. I don't know what Marriott was doing here. But a bit later I saw the two of them together, talking. And I don't know whether I ought to get in touch with that detective and mention it, or if it isn't worthwhile. If I hadn't made the man look rather a fool I think I'd get in touch with him as a matter of course, even though it can't be of any importance. But I don't like the idea of giving him a chance to make me look a fool too."

The door opened and coffee was brought in. The tray was put down on the desk in front of Ramsden and the girl who had brought it departed. While she was in the room both Ramsden and Andrew were silent, but as she left Ramsden pushed a cup towards Andrew, and Andrew said, "You saw Marriott and Greenslade talking together, you're quite sure of that?"

"Yes, yes," Ramsden said impatiently. "I've no idea what they were talking about and it looked quite normal to me. I mean, Marriott didn't look as if he was afraid for his life. But the question is, do you think I ought to do anything about it?"

"Why not?" Andrew said, "it can't do any harm."

"It's just that I don't like the idea of talking to that man and telling him I made a mistake. He may try to make out he believes I did it on purpose."

"Why not get in touch with some other man then?" Andrew said. "The man in charge of the inquiry is called Barrymore. You could ask for him."

Ramsden's keen grey eyes studied Andrew for a moment. He drank some coffee, then leant back in his chair, still watching Andrew with a steady but faintly puzzled stare.

"I believe you think the matter *is* important," Ramsden said. "I don't understand that myself."

"I've no idea if it is or it isn't," Andrew answered. "It's just that when you're dealing with a thing like murder it's really best to recognize that the smallest thing may have its significance."

"You're interested, aren't you, in the fact that Marriott and Greenslade were in here together?" Ramsden said.

Andrew had an uncomfortable feeling that words were being put into his mouth, that things he had never had any intention of saying were being accepted as what he meant and then were being challenged.

He countered the feeling by saying, "I think it's you who are interested in that, Ramsden."

"Yes, I am," Ramsden admitted. "I can't help being interested in everything that's happened to Marriott during the last few days. And I suppose you're right that I ought to get in touch with that man—you said his name was Barrymore, didn't you? —and tell him about this very small matter which he'll probably think is just a way of wasting his time. As a matter of fact, it's what Alison said I ought to do, but I don't think she was really thinking about it. She's so wrapped up in this affair of Caroline and Owen that she doesn't pay attention to anything else to speak of."

He spooned sugar into his coffee and smiled in a way that completely changed his sharp-featured, rather expressionless face.

"You can understand it, I expect," he went on. "She's known for quite a while that they were putting off their marriage because of the way we've let ourselves become so dependent on Caroline for looking after Alison, and at the back of our minds, of course, she and I have been feeling dreadfully guilty about it, and yet we just let things drift on. Then only the other day we made up our minds we'd got to tell the girl to get on and marry the man before the affair was hopelessly ruined. I can't tell you what a load off our minds it's been, deciding that. Caroline's radiant. She's wandering around in a dream of utter happiness. I haven't seen anything like it since I was her age myself and fell in love with Alison. I only hope to God Owen's worth it. If she's back home in a year or two, wanting a divorce, I'll never forgive him."

It sounded as if he did not know how to stop himself talking.

"However," he continued, "I'm rather wandering away from what I started to say. I meant to say Alison thinks we ought to tell the police about Marriott and Greenslade meeting here the other morning. Greenslade's rather a friend of hers. He's been very good to her since her accident. But I don't believe she was even thinking about what she was saying, because the next moment she was talking about what a pity it was that Caroline and Owen were insisting on getting married in a registry office instead of making a fine church wedding of the affair and how she'd have loved to help Caroline choose her wedding dress. Well, I mean to say, how do you keep your head and think clearly when it's murder one minute and marriage the next?"

Andrew agreed that it was not the simplest of problems, but repeated that he did not think there could be any harm in telling Superintendent Barrymore about the meeting between Kenneth Marriott and Walter Greenslade in the library. It was only after he and Ramsden had finished their coffee and separated, and Andrew was strolling towards the staff club, that it dawned on him that he was anxious on his own account that Ramsden should tell the Superintendent about having seen the two men together. Andrew's own problem, until Ramsden had said positively that he had seen this, was that he was not sure that the two people who had been talking in the alcove next to his on his first morning in the library, saying strange things about possessing 'a knife,' had been Marriott and Greenslade. Now the responsibility for saying that it had been was shifted onto Ramsden's shoulders. If in the end he did nothing about it, that would not be Andrew's fault, and now it could not be said that Andrew had deliberately kept something back which the police ought to have been told.

He spent that evening with Walter. They met by chance after the afternoon session in the Botany Department, and Walter asked him home to dinner with him. Andrew's first impulse was to discover that, sad to say, he had another engagement elsewhere. For the moment his mind was haunted by the feeling that only too probably Walter Greenslade was a murderer and that dining with a murderer was not the most attractive of prospects. But after only a moment something seemed to click in his mind, allowing him to remember that he had no evidence at all that Walter had ever raised his hand against anyone. He might or might not have been paying blackmail to Marriott, who was connected somehow with the murder of Judd, or else why should Marriott's statement that he had a knife be of any importance to either of them? But Walter had not murdered Marriott. At the time of the murder he had been at a dinner of the Botanical Association, possibly making his after-dinner speech. He had a perfect alibi. And after all he was an old friend, someone whom Andrew had known for years. You did not lie to your old friends about imaginary engagements merely because he might have committed some imaginary murder.

Andrew had been in Walter's house before on an earlier visit to Knotlington. It was a semi-detached Victorian building, much larger than Walter, living by himself since the death of his sister, had any need of. But he seemed to have clung to it out of sentiment. At first, when Walter took Andrew into the big, dignified sitting-room with its high ceiling, its black marble fireplace, its velvet-covered sofa and chairs and solid mahogany furniture, he thought that nothing had changed in it since he had seen it last. Then a memory came back to him that at one end of the room there used to hang a portrait of Veronica Greenslade, which was not there now. Instead a reproduction Monet of some irises in a garden hung there. Andrew had never much cared for the portrait of Veronica, which had given her a look of dominant strength, almost of fierceness, which was quite unlike her. She had been a gentle, docile woman, quietly intelligent. Because he had not cared for the picture, Andrew had never spoken about it, but now he realised that of course it had been the work of Carl Judd. If some of the things that Andrew had been hearing about him were true, it was not surprising, he thought, that Walter had removed it.

Walter was so fortunate as to have acquired an excellent housekeeper, an elderly woman whose cooking, to go by the meal that she provided that evening—some very good soup, some roast lamb, and some raspberries and cream—could hardly have been bettered. But Walter appeared to have very little appetite and though he gave liberal helpings of everything to Andrew, gave himself very little. Remembering how at their first meeting in the staff club it had struck him that Walter looked ill, Andrew thought that he now looked even more haggard than he did then. Walter's long, smooth, bland face had a weary blankness about it. Besides looking ill, he looked very tired and deeply depressed.

He talked about the conference, about what he had found interesting and what, it seemed to him, had been merely the precocious work of the young who were taking themselves far too seriously to make any impression on a mature scientist. He sounded peevish about it, which suggested jealousy of the energy and hopefulness of youth, but what most struck Andrew about the way he talked was that he seemed to be making a point of avoiding mentioning the death of Kenneth Marriott. He spoke of how good it felt to talk to someone who was actually older than he was himself, and then, apologizing to Andrew in case this was not the most tactful of things to have said, started talking of the old days when he had been a student of Andrew's, and how he had always been drawn to people who had had experience of life far beyond his own.

Sitting over coffee when the table had been cleared, he said, "Yes, it's true, you know, Andrew, the only woman I ever really fell in love with was ten years older than I was myself. When I asked her to marry me she only laughed at me. She told me I'd got a mother-fixation and that it would never do. I daresay she was right—in fact, I'm sure she was. My mother died when I was ten and I suppose I went on looking for her ever after. It may have been why Veronica meant so much to me. Actually she was younger than I was, about two years, but she was far more mature than I was and she had a way of looking after me which I suppose it was childish of me to come to expect. You can't think how I miss her, and my God, how I hate that devil Judd for what he did to her! She was the sweetest, dearest woman and he destroyed her. He drove her right over the edge. But it wasn't murder! Oh no, not murder, it was just a quiet way of making her life not worth living any more. Isn't it extraordinary that you can do that to a person, yet there's no way you can be punished for it? It isn't a crime. All it is is evil, but there aren't any laws against evil."

Walter's voice had been rising, with growing excitement in it, and the lines of his smooth, calm face had become more deeply drawn.

"Veronica was in love with Judd, I understand," Andrew said.

"Passionately, passionately!" Walter exclaimed. "And he led her on, not because he had the least feeling for her, it was because it gave him something he wanted from her when he was painting her. And like a fool, I didn't understand that. I actually commissioned him to paint that last portrait of her. I didn't understand what I was doing. It would have been a wonderful portrait, I believe, of a woman in love. You should have seen her when they were together, how she changed, how her whole personality blossomed and came to life. And then he calmly told her that he didn't need her any more, he'd got all he needed from her. And a few nights later she swallowed a whole bottleful of sleeping pills and when I got home—I'd been away for a few days—I found her dead. She left a letter behind, telling me what had happened."

He drew his breath in a deep sigh.

"I suppose you're thinking I ought not to have encouraged her in an affair with a married man, and now it's so easy to look back and say that of course I shouldn't," he said. "But I believed he was really in love with her and that his marriage didn't mean much and that there was no reason why he shouldn't get a divorce and he and Veronica get married. Of course, the truth about things was, I believe now, that he never cared for anyone but his wife. He wasn't faithful to her, but after his fashion he loved her."

"Do you think it was Margaret Judd who slashed the portrait of Veronica?" Andrew asked.

Walter took off his glasses and began thoughtfully polishing them with his handkerchief. His eyes, without the glasses to shield them, had a disturbingly defenceless look.

"I don't know," he muttered. "Probably. Possibly. Perhaps not. I haven't the least idea. Have some more coffee."

# Six

ANDREW SUDDENLY BEGAN to feel anxious to get back to the privacy of his room in the hostel. Standing up, he said that he was sure that Walter had had a tiring day and that it was time for him to leave.

Walter looked surprised at the abruptness of it, but he did not argue. He drove Andrew to the hostel and on the way hardly spoke. When he stopped the car at the gates he said that no doubt he and Andrew would see each other again next day; then, when Andrew had got out of the car, he drove off at a speed which somehow suggested that until then he had been holding himself back, perhaps because a man of Andrew's age might dislike going any faster. Andrew pushed open the big gates and went up to the door of the hostel.

There was a porter on duty inside and as Andrew came in he addressed him: "Professor Basnett?"

"Yes," Andrew said.

"There's a lady come to see you," the porter said. "I think she's still here. She said she'd wait. Unless she's gone without I noticed her, she's in the common room. She didn't leave her name."

Andrew felt dismay. There was no lady in Knotlington whom he felt much inclined to meet at that hour. Reluctantly he went towards the common room, a big room on the ground floor which overlooked the gardens at the back of the building. It had tall windows, over which the curtains had not been drawn. They made shiny glass rectangles of darkness in the pale grey walls, in which the chairs and tables and bookcases in the room were reflected. In one of them too there was a reflection of a woman with abundant yellow hair. It was piled up in a knot on her head instead of falling down in a pony-tail, but Andrew recognized her at once as Margaret Judd.

She was sitting on a sofa against the wall, looking dreamy and unaware of her surroundings, but as soon as she saw Andrew she stood up quickly and held out a hand to him. He took it and they sat down on the sofa, Andrew looking questioningly at her and she dropping her gaze to the floor as if, now that they had met, she wanted to avoid making any contact with him. It was almost as if it was not he whom she had come there to meet and she found it awkward to have accidentally encountered him. It crossed his mind that this might be the case, but then she suddenly looked up at him, her eyes meeting his with singular brightness, and he no longer had any doubt that it was with him that she wanted to talk.

"Please," she said in a low voice as if she were afraid that someone among the few people still sitting in the common room might overhear her, "do you think I'm a murderer? Tell me the truth. Whatever I say, is that what you're going to believe?"

Andrew felt very embarrassed. He stroked one side of his jaw in a nervous way, crossed one leg over the other, and for the first time for many years wished that he had not given up smoking. A cigarette would have helped him over the next few minutes.

"I believe what a person has to say on a subject like that doesn't carry much weight," he said. "It's other things that count."

"Yes, of course," she said. "It was a silly thing for me to say. It was just that I didn't know how else to begin. There are some things I want to tell you and to ask you, but it's so difficult to go straight into it without any preliminaries. I went yesterday to talk to the police, you see, and I took for granted they'd believe me and they didn't. They didn't exactly say so, but I could see they didn't, and now I don't know what to do. So I thought of coming to you to see if you would help me. But of course it's too late in the evening and you're probably tired and won't want to listen to me at all. I've a way of forgetting that other people often don't like to stay up late. I often don't go to bed till two or three in the morning. I don't sleep much and I hate lying there wide awake, knowing sleep isn't going to come. It's how it's been ever since Carl's death and really it doesn't worry me much. I'm quite used to it. But I forget that other people like their eight hours. You look tired. Shall I go away?"

She still spoke in a half-whispering and hurried way.

"Mrs. Judd, if I can help you in any way," Andrew said, "of course I will, but please don't think I'm likely to be able to. I believe that nephew of mine gave you the idea that I know a lot about all sorts of strange things, but honestly it isn't true."

"All right, it isn't true," she said. She gave a little smile as if the fact that he had not sent her away, refusing to listen to her, were reassuring. "You'd say that, of course, because you're the unpretentious kind of person who'd never claim to be able to do things that perhaps he couldn't. And I'm not trying to get you to commit yourself to doing anything you think you can't. But if you'd just listen to me, and if you can, advise me . . ."

"I'll do my best," Andrew said. "And at least I believe I'm a fairly good listener."

A bright smile, as if of gratitude, flashed across her face, then faded.

"Well, you see, yesterday evening I went to the police." Her voice was as soft as ever. "I'd suddenly got it into my head that that was the right thing to do. I thought it would be best if I told them a certain thing before they found it out for themselves. If they did that, I thought, they'd be sure to suspect me of some rather dreadful things. But it didn't help at all. I think they thought it was suspicious, my coming to talk to them."

Andrew interrupted, "Mrs. Judd. I think I ought to tell you that I believe I know what you're going to tell me. I saw that man Barrymore yesterday evening, soon after you'd been to see him—I'd been having dinner with Giles Farmoor—and Barrymore told us why you'd been."

Her forehead wrinkled in a troubled frown.

"He did? And I thought it would be confidential. Wasn't that mean of him?"

"Perhaps it was, but I shouldn't worry about it since you want to tell me about it yourself."

"Oh, of course that's true, but still somehow I thought . . . Well, never mind. It just shows how stupid I am about things like this. You know, when Carl was killed I did everything wrong. I made them suspect me by trying to convince them I wasn't jealous of Veronica and his other women. They thought that was so unnatural it must be pretence. And so it was to some extent, but it would have been so humiliating to admit how hurt I was by the things he did. Well, that isn't what I was going to talk about, as you know. It was the money I've been paying Gwen. You see, when Stephen was sent to prison she was left penniless, and I was certain he was innocent and that I'd got to do what I could to help her. So I've been paying her five hundred pounds a month just to keep her going. And that was what I wanted the police to understand, that it was just to keep her going, it wasn't blackmail."

"And they don't believe you?"

"I don't know what they made of it. They didn't understand why I'd come to speak to them. They were sure there was something wrong about it, I mean, that I wouldn't have done it if I hadn't been trying to cover up something. They were reasonably courteous, but I could see they thought I was a fool, trying to make them believe a story like that. As I suppose I was. I suppose it was very unconvincing."

"I can tell you what they did as soon as you left, or perhaps it was being done while you were still in the police station," Andrew said. "They phoned up Mrs. Sharland and asked her if she'd been receiving money from you for the last couple of years. And she said no, she'd never had anything from you."

Margaret Judd gave a deep sigh. It had a sound of hopelessness, yet the gaze that she had fixed on Andrew's face was searching and doubting, rather than despairing.

"She really said that?" she said.

"So I understood from Barrymore," Andrew answered.

"How she must hate me!"

She dropped her face into her hands, hiding it, but the tension of her fragile body betrayed how deeply she felt fear, or perhaps it was anger, or a bitter kind of hurt.

"Have you ever known anyone who really hated you?" she asked after a moment, letting her hands fall and looking up at him, and he saw that there were tears in her dark eyes.

"Come to think of it, I don't believe I have," Andrew said. "Acute dislike of course, and jealousy—you couldn't get through an academic career without encountering those—and perhaps contempt because you weren't just that bit more successful than you were. Oh, naturally, all sorts of disagreeable things. But hatred, anything as intense as that, no, I don't think so."

"I didn't think I had either until this moment," she said. "She was ready enough to take the help when I offered it, but now . . . She couldn't say I hadn't helped her really quite generously, except out of pure hatred, could she? It frightens me. If you can be as evil as that, what might you be capable of doing next?"

"You hate her too, don't you?" Andrew said.

"I don't believe I've ever hated anybody," she said. "Is that unnatural? Do most people hate the people they can't manage to love? Perhaps I'm too cold-blooded for either. As far as I can remember, I haven't really loved many people, but I haven't hated them either. Some people might say, I suppose, that I can't really have loved Carl because I wasn't jealous enough of him to want to murder him or his women. But I truly loved him. Do you believe me?"

"Why not?" Andrew said. "From what I've heard of him he doesn't sound what I'd call a very lovable person, but he may have been what you needed. But tell me something—it puzzles me that in all of his portraits of you he makes you a brawny, hardworking peasant of a woman, and it doesn't seem to me that that's a very perceptive portrayal of what you are."

She gave a brief laugh. "Of course not. But he didn't mean those pictures as portraits of me. I think they were portraits of his mother. He was illegitimate, you know, and she brought him up by herself, and that meant she had to work very hard indeed to look after him as well as herself. I think she must have been a very fine, brave woman. And I think the only reason he fell in love with me was that my hair was the same colour as hers. But really he always wanted me to look after him. He'd have liked to give up his job in the University and do nothing but paint, but for him to have been able to do that I'd have had to get a job that brought in enough to keep the two of us. My father was still alive then, I hadn't inherited anything from him, and we were always hard up." She suddenly brought her hands down with a slap on her knees. "Oh, why am I talking like this? What I want, Professor Basnett, is to ask you to go and talk to Gwen and try to get her to admit that I did give her that money. Five hundred a month—that's six thousand pounds a year and if it isn't wealth for her, it's quite a lot of money. She can't be so mean as to go on swearing I didn't give it to her."

Andrew had known that sooner or later she was going to ask

him to do something for her. There could be no other reason for
her visit to him this evening. It might have been something that
he would have found still more difficult or disagreeable than
what she had just asked him to do. He did not mind the idea of
having another talk with Gwen Sharland. But being an honest
man, or at least as reasonably honest as most, he felt impelled to
point out certain difficulties to her.

"I don't mind trying to persuade Mrs. Sharland to admit she's
been getting money from you," he said, "but I don't believe for
a moment she'll listen to me. For one thing, if she does admit it,
isn't it going to look as if she's been extorting that money from
you? In other words, that it's been blackmail. And that's going
to look as bad for her as it will for you."

She gave him a long, startled look.

"So I was wrong about you," she said. "I thought I could trust
you not to leap to that conclusion."

"Oh, I haven't leapt to any conclusion," he said, "except that I
don't believe for a moment she'll listen to me. Once having
taken the stand that she hasn't had the money, it's going to be
very difficult for her to change her story. And I don't believe I'm
specially good at persuading anyone of anything they don't feel
inclined to admit. Haven't you any proof that you gave her the
money? How did you pay her? By cheque, or was it by cash?"

She gave another of her deep sighs. "Sometimes one, sometimes the other. I think it could be proved that I gave her money
from time to time during the last two years, though it couldn't
be proved why I gave it to her. Will that help me or not?"

"I'm not sure. If she sticks to it that you didn't give her any
money and then it can be shown that you did, it won't look too
good for her."

"But I don't want to make things bad for her."

"Even if it's rather important for your own sake?"

"I don't know, I don't know." She wrung her hands together.
"Things have been so fearful for her. She's suffered so terribly
and really she's been so brave."

"You're very generous."

He had not made up his mind whether or not he believed that this was true. If the money of which they were talking had been extorted from her by threats and not freely given, the generosity could be part of an act. A tinge of irony must have got into his voice when he spoke, for there was something sharply sardonic about what she said next.

"Oh yes, I'm generosity itself. I'm glad you think so. But if I gave her that money because I was compelled to do so, because of the power she had over me, knowing I'd killed Carl, then it doesn't matter much, does it, whether or not it was blackmail? It's such a small crime compared with murder."

He nodded. "I suppose you're right."

She stood up suddenly.

"All right, if you don't want to help me, we needn't say any more about it. Forget I came here. I imagine you're right that there's nothing much you can do, even if you'd like to. I don't know why she should hate me as much as she does, but there it is, she does. I suppose she honestly thinks I killed Carl and have let Stephen suffer for it. I expect in her place I'd have felt the same."

"You've a strange way of believing in the honesty of other people," he said. "I believe, if I were you and assuming that what you've told me is true, I'd have been trying to work out what she had to gain by denying that she ever accepted money from you."

"Oh, I'm doing that," she said. "I shall probably stay awake all night, trying to find the answer to that question. Well, thank you for listening to me. I know I shouldn't have come, but I thought that perhaps—just perhaps—but I realise it was too much to ask of a stranger. The funny thing is, I don't feel we're strangers. I wonder if you often give people that feeling. It's as if I've known you quite a long time. But I'll leave you in peace now. No, don't see me out, my car's in the road."

She moved quickly and while he was still considering

whether or not to take her at her word and leave her to make her
way out to her car, she had shot out through the door and disappeared.

Andrew had stood up but now sat down again and leaning
back in his chair, gazing dreamily up at the ceiling, tried to rid
himself of a feeling of failure. He ought, he felt sure, to have
been able to do more for the woman that he had. Unfortunately
he still did not know how far he believed her. He supposed it
was true, since it could be proved by the cheques that she had
signed, that she had given Gwen Sharland money. But whether
or not it had been out of sheer generosity or because the other
woman had been able to squeeze it out of her by some power
that she had over her, he had not begun to think. Really the only
thing for him to do, he thought, was to go to see Gwen Sharland
in the morning and see what he felt after a talk with her.

Meanwhile, he realised, he was extremely tired. The feeling
had come on him suddenly, as it often did these days. Old age
had a way of attacking him without warning, striking him down
from a reasonably active and thoughtful state of mind to drowsy
weariness. The only thing for him to do at the moment, he
thought, was go to bed. Then in the morning, if he still felt the
same way about it, he would go to see Gwen Sharland. But of
course there was always the possibility that by then he might
have reverted to the idea that the best thing for him to do was to
return to London.

In the morning he got up, showered and shaved and ate his
ration of cheese. While he was shaving, looking at himself in the
mirror, he caught himself murmuring:

> *"There is a Reaper, whose name is Death,*
> *And with his sickle keen . . ."*

With his razor keen at that moment he made a little nick in
his chin. As blood spurted he interrupted Longfellow to swear.
The bleeding lasted only a moment and as he mopped it up with
a towel, seeing a red smear appear on it, he thought how threat-

ening a thing the colour of blood is, even in the most diminutive quantities. No wonder that blood red had become the symbol of revolutionary violence. The trouble about the song, "The Red Flag," of course, was that for reasons mysterious in the extreme the tune selected for it was one of the most charming of old German folk songs: "*Oh, Tannenbaum, oh, Tannenbaum, wie grün sind deine Blätter . . .*" In his early youth Andrew, with a few friends, had more than once gone on long treks through the dark green forests of southern Germany, not yet aware of what Hitler was preparing for the world or how, for his generation, the memory of those long peaceful pine-scented days would be loathesomely stained by the red of blood, and of more blood, and of horror and terror. . . .

The little snip on his chin was stinging. No doubt that abominable Reaper was at work, bringing back to Andrew's mind, after a quiet night's sleep which might have made him forget it, the fact that all too much blood had been spilled in Knotlington and that he had promised Margaret Judd to try to help in the operation of mopping up, useless as this was likely to be.

After he had had breakfast, he set off to see Gwen Sharland.

The morning was cloudy and cool, far less attractive than the day before had been, and as windy and depressingly grey as he remembered midsummer days in the Midlands could be. It was nearly half past ten when he reached the crescent where Gwen lived. He climbed the few steps to her door and rang her bell, but had no answer. He rang the bell again several times before giving up and going down the steps to the street and standing there thoughtfully for a minute or two before deciding what to do next.

She might have gone out to do her shopping for the coming weekend and could be gone for an hour or more. Or she might have gone out to meet a friend or to do almost anything. Waiting around was not going to be any use. Fulfilling his promise to Margaret Judd would have to wait. But it might be pleasant, even though the morning was not very sunny, to stroll once

more through the Botanic Garden. Crossing the main road to
the gates of the garden he went through them and took the path
this time that would lead him to the lily pool.

It was a small, formal pool, the centre of a paved area in
which yellow flag irises and the big, dock-like leaves of the water
plantain were growing. Andrew recognised the narrow, dark
leaves of the water hawthorn, even though it was not in bloom.
As a professor of botany he was always expected to recognise
even the most exotic of plants, whereas he generally felt pleased
with himself if he could identify any of the commoner weeds in
some friend's garden. His work in fact had been mainly bio-
chemical, the product of laboratory studies.

That did not mean that he did not love the beauties of the
plant world, and now, finding a seat overlooking the pool, he
settled down to enjoy it. In the afternoon, he thought, he would
carry out his plan of returning to London. But for the present
he had to face the fact that the tall, slim figure of a woman
walking slowly towards him was Gwen Sharland and that unless she failed to notice him and strolled straight past, he would
have to speak to her after all.

She did not fail to notice him. Approaching him she smiled as
if she were glad to see him, and as he hurriedly got to his feet to
greet her, she sat down on the bench beside him. He sat down
too and remarked that the weather was disappointing. She
agreed with him, but said that last night's weather forecast on
television for today promised better things to come. Then she
fell silent and Andrew also suddenly could not think of anything to say. It seemed as if there would be no rational way of
breaking the silence that descended on them. Then they both
began to speak at the same time.

Andrew said, "I called at your house just a little while
ago. . . ."

Gwen Sharland said, "I've been hoping to see you again sometime. . . ."

For some reason the clash of their two voices struck them both as funny and they both began to laugh.

Then Gwen sat back on the bench, folded her hands on her lap and said, "You've actually been at my flat looking for me, have you? I'm so sorry I wasn't there. Was it about something important?"

"Well, fairly important, I suppose," Andrew said, "though to be honest with you, I was a little relieved to find you weren't in."

"And then you meet me here," she said. "That's very hard on you. It's something to do with that money Margaret claims she gave me, is that it? And you're horribly put out because you've probably promised that you'll talk to me about it."

"You're very perceptive," he said. "But how do you know so much?"

"I don't, of course. I was just guessing," she said. "But the police have been to question me about some money that Margaret claims she gave me, and I thought very likely she'd got you drilled into doing some questioning too. Isn't that what happened?"

"You could put it like that, I suppose," Andrew said. "It's true she wanted me to persuade you into admitting you'd accepted a fair amount of money from her, and I gave her a sort of promise that I'd try to do it. But I also told her I didn't expect I'd have the slightest chance of success."

"That was sensible of you," she said.

"You still say you didn't receive any money from her?" Andrew said. "I believe that's what you told the police."

"Of course."

"Because it wasn't true that you did?"

"Naturally."

"I wonder, then, why she should stick to this story that she's been paying you five hundred pounds a month. It's a substantial sum."

"Yes, indeed. But I don't happen to need it."

"You know, I feel extraordinarily discourteous, talking to you about it at all," he said. "Money is one of our great taboos, we all carefully avoid talking about how much we earn, or if it isn't earned, how much we have or where it comes from."

"Oh, I know. You'd find it easier to ask me how many lovers I've had while I've been living all alone as a pseudo-widow than anything about the source of my income. I'm sorry it's so difficult for you. But you really needn't worry. Margaret, of course, is tactlessness itself. When she persuaded you to try to discover what I live on she won't have thought for a moment how insensitive she was being. She's a really awful woman."

"So she's right that you hate her."

"Is that what she said?"

"Yes."

"I suppose it's true. Half-true. If I've ever hated anyone, it's Margaret. Only hatred is such a shattering emotion that I'm frightened of it. If I really let myself feel it, I don't know what it might do to me. Would I take to murder too? You do realize she's a murderess, don't you? And she's got away with it while my husband rots in prison. You do understand, don't you, that in the circumstances it's difficult not to hate?"

"You're saying about the same thing she said on the subject."

"Really? She understands how much I hate her?"

"Oh, yes."

"And yet I've tried not to hate her. Honestly I have. That may be only, as I was saying, because I'm scared of what it might do to me and not really because I'm too virtuous to feel anything so violent. I suppose I'm frightened of most intense feelings, the loving and tender ones as well as the cruel ones. Isn't that strange? It means I'm very inhibited, doesn't it? And that's a thing we all despise now. We're supposed to be able to let our feelings rip."

Andrew looked absently across the lily pool to where a sleek grey dove was strutting to and fro on the paving on the far side of it, declaring in a husky voice, so it seemed to him, that papa

was dead. It said so over and over again. It had never occurred to
Andrew before that that was what doves say: "Papa is dead,
papa is dead. . . ."

How absurd to start thinking of such a thing just then. What
he really wanted to think about was which of the two women,
Margaret Judd or Gwen Sharland, was lying, because of course
one of them was.

The way that Gwen had led the conversation away from the
subject of whether or not Margaret had been paying her a substantial sum of money every month made him inclined to believe that it was Gwen who was lying. He decided not to let
himself be led away again from the question of what he wanted
to know.

"If I may go on talking about money, in spite of that taboo
we've mentioned," he said, "may I ask you if there's any truth in
Mrs. Judd's statement to me that without help from her you'd
have been in great difficulties financially?"

"Ask anything you like," she answered. "I won't take offence.
But I may not give you a very rewarding answer."

"Which is a way of telling me not to ask the question."

"Perhaps it is. But not exactly. For instance, I don't mind
telling you that I've an adequate income of my own and have
never needed Margaret's help. Whether or not I'd have accepted
it if I'd needed it, I don't know. I don't know how much pride I
have, since it's never really been tested. But it happens that my
father was a very successful surgeon and left me quite a lot of
money, so even when Stephen went to prison I wasn't penniless."

The dove chose that moment to proclaim, "Papa is dead, papa
is dead."

"Now that's a very extraordinary thing," Andrew said, looking thoughtfully across the pool at the bird there.

"What is?" Gwen Sharland asked.

"Only that Mrs. Judd's father was a successful surgeon too
who left her quite a lot of money."

"A strange coincidence," she said.

"Yes, I would say so, distinctly strange," he agreed.

"So you don't believe me." Her voice was suddenly mocking.

"I don't really see why I shouldn't," he said. "Coincidences happen by the dozen all the time and they always seem to one strange, but really they're quite commonplace."

"Oh, don't pretend!" she said. "You don't believe me."

She suddenly stood up and seemed about to walk away. But then she stood still, looking down at him.

"You're quite right, of course," she said, "I've been lying."

It took him by surprise, not that she had been lying, of which he had been fairly sure, but that she should so soon have admitted it.

"My father was a schoolmaster in St. Hilda's School in Knotlington," she said. "His salary was barely adequate and he had nothing to leave to me. My mother died two years before he did and his pension stopped when he died. It didn't help me. But I'm not penniless because I've got a job. I work for a typing agency. It suits me quite well, because I can work at home, in my own time, and I like that. But the pay's very poor, as you can imagine. So the five hundred a month that Margaret's been paying me has made an enormous difference. But I still hate the woman. Can you understand that, that I should accept money from someone I detest and despise as much as I do her?"

Andrew turned his palms outwards in a gesture of doubt.

"I'm fortunate," he said, "I've never been tested."

"D'you know why I accepted it?"

"I suppose it just could be it wasn't exactly a case of accepting it, but of extorting it."

"Blackmail, you mean?"

"Well, was it?" At a time of crisis, Andrew's voice had a way of becoming remarkably calm.

Her face turned curiously pale. "Bastard!" she said softly.

"Well now, wasn't that what you wanted me to say?" he asked.

"I'm not a blackmailer."

"I'm so glad," he said.

She hit one fist fiercely against the palm of the other hand. It was as if she would have preferred to hit him. "You don't believe me."

"I haven't said that," Andrew said. "I'm only a little puzzled why she should have been paying you a considerable amount and you should have been accepting it if something in the nature of blackmail never arose. But if you could explain to me how and why it happened it would be quite a load off my mind."

"All right, I'll tell you." She turned away from him, gazing across the pool and over the long sweep of grass beyond it. "She offered me that money, saying she was sure I'd need it and sympathizing with me with great crocodile tears because my husband was in prison, but never saying a word about believing I knew she'd killed her husband. It made me laugh. Well, not exactly laugh, not out loud, but inside myself, because she was so frightened. She must have thought, I don't know why, that I'd evidence of what she'd done. We were so nice to one another that day, you'd have laughed too if you'd been there to see it. And I took the money and it's helped me very much ever since, because I thought she deserved to pay it, even though I'd never asked for it. She did kill Carl, you know. I'm certain of it."

"Have you that evidence she thinks you've got?" Andrew asked.

"That would be telling! Suppose I haven't, then that would be the end of a nice income, and suppose I have, then I ought to have taken it to the police long ago and got my husband freed, oughtn't I? And perhaps I'm not all that eager to get my husband back. Perhaps I'd sooner have my five hundred a month!"

"Stop it!" Andrew said. "I don't know how much of what you've told me is lies, but a good deal of it is. I'm sure of that, and I don't much like it."

"You don't much like me, do you?"

"Why should I, considering you can't be bothered to be honest with me?"

She sat down again on the bench, turned to him and smiled. "Andrew, you really want me to be honest, don't you?" she said. "It really upsets you to be told lies. But the truth is, I haven't told you any; or anyway, not a lot. That woman killed her husband. That's clear as day to everyone. She really did, you know. She'd been smothering her feelings of jealousy for years and at last it came to the breaking point, and seeing him at work on that portrait of Veronica, even after Veronica was dead, was more than she could stand and she stabbed him and slashed the portrait. I know it because of the blood on Stephen's pullover."

"I thought it was that that proved the case against him."

"Oh yes, but how stupid that idea was. As if he'd have left it there in a drawer if it was really Carl's blood got onto him after a murder. What really happened is that Stephen went in to see Carl to patch things up after a quarrel they'd had, and he found him dead and the picture slashed from top to bottom and the knife missing. And he had an idea he might be able to do something for Carl and he turned him over and got blood on himself. And when he saw it he panicked and came running home to me and told me all about it. But that little devil Marriott saw him come running blindly out of the house and told the police about it and they found Stephen's fingerprints all over the place in the studio, and when he was questioned he broke down hopelessly. He's a very gentle, nervous sort of man who couldn't stand up to any pressure, and the police put plenty of pressure on him. Why hadn't he telephoned them straight away when he found the body, they wanted to know. And he couldn't tell them, nor could I, except that we wanted to keep out of the whole thing. But anyhow they'd made up their minds about him before they ever started questioning him. And only a little while later, before the trial, Margaret offered me money and to me that clinched it. She made me promise not to tell anyone I was getting it, but that isn't actually what's kept me quiet about it, it was simply that I didn't think the right time had come to talk about it. The right time, if that's what you're going to ask me about, is the time that will get her convicted of murder."

"And this is it?"

"It might be."

"You want me to do something about it, of course."

"Are you up to it?"

It was Andrew's turn to stand up and stroll to the paved edge of the pool.

"I'll think about it."

"I want more than that."

"I'm sorry, I'm just a plant physiologist. My interest in life is in the compatibility of proteins. I'm not a detective."

"Didn't you tell Margaret you'd think about it? I want more than you promised her."

He gave a slight shake of his head, "It's a good deal to promise, you know, that one'll think about a thing. I don't think about many things these days. It's too hard work."

She stood up again and once more hissed softly, "Bastard!" Then she turned and walked quickly away.

He stayed where he was for some time until he could no longer hear the tapping of her heels on the pathway; then, walking slowly, he followed her, being careful not to overtake her. By the time that he reached the gateway out of the gardens she was out of sight.

Reaching the street, he stood still, wondering if there was any chance of catching a taxi here. No taxis came by, but after some minutes a bus came along, going in the direction of the university. He climbed on to it and stayed on until it reached the stop nearest to the staff club. He was looking forward to a drink and some lunch, and after that perhaps he might attend the seminar on the pigments of the chloroplasts that was going to be held that afternoon. Alternatively he might return to his room in the hostel, pack his small suitcase, and go home.

He went in at the entrance to the staff club and found himself face to face with someone to whom for the moment he could not

put a name, though he knew the young man's face at once. With
increasing age his tendency to forget names was growing on
him deplorably.

"Professor Basnett!" the young man exclaimed. "I rather
hoped I might meet you. That's why I came in. I was just thinking of giving up, but now that we've met perhaps you'll have a
drink with me."

"Thank you," Andrew said. "That's very nice of you. I'd like
that."

Now who the devil, he asked himself, is this?

# Seven

HE SOLVED THE PROBLEM while, having sat down at one of the tables, he was waiting for the drinks to be brought. The young man was Owen Phillips, the fiancé of Caroline Ramsden. But there had been a remarkable change in the young man's face since Andrew had met him in the Ramsdens' house. It looked far older. The glow of happiness had altogether disappeared from it. It had even a trace of grimness. If this was his real personality showing itself, Andrew thought that perhaps Caroline did not know what she was in for. A moody character, apparently, who might not be too easy to live with.

However, when Phillips arrived with the drinks and sat down facing Andrew, the grimness had faded. There was merely a look of worry on his face, an expression that looked rather like apology.

"I'm sorry," he began at once, "I probably oughtn't to have bothered you—with my affairs, you know. But the Ramsdens

seem to think a lot of you, so I thought you were someone I
could consult. But I realise it's taking rather a lot for granted."

"I hardly know the Ramsdens," Andrew said. "Mrs. Ramsden
was a student of mine many years ago, and Gregory Ramsden I
met for the first time the day before yesterday. I'm glad if they
have a high opinion of me, but I can't think how I can have
deserved it."

"Is that really so?" Phillips asked doubtingly. "Mrs. Ramsden
spoke as if she knew you quite well."

"I think students remember their lecturers much better than
the lecturers remember them," Andrew said, "specially if the
lecturer is in his way attentive. As I remember it, she wasn't
very bright and I gave her some extra coaching when the exams
were looming ahead. In its way, it may have meant a good deal
to her. But what has that to do with why you want to talk to
me?"

"I just thought you might be able to talk to the Ramsdens, to
get Caroline—well, to get her to see reason."

"Is she being unreasonable then?"

"That's how I see it."

Andrew felt fairly sure that he knew what was coming. "She
won't go to Toronto, is that it?"

"Yes."

"But you're still going?"

"I don't know. That's the hell of it. I can't decide. What ought
one to do in a situation like this? I thought if someone like you
would talk to Mrs Ramsden . . ." He broke off. Instead of appearing older than when Andrew had seen him before, the
young man looked not only very young but very vulnerable.

"Has Caroline actually broken off your engagement?" he
asked.

"It seems to me that's what it comes to. She says she can't
leave her mother, but that I mustn't give up the job I've just got,
and she talks vaguely about coming out to join me sometime
later. But of course she won't. If she won't come now, she won't

come at all. But she just doesn't want to take the responsibility of being the one to break off the engagement, she wants to leave that to me. Or else she wants me to stay in Knotlington, but without being to blame for putting pressure on me to do that. And I don't know what to do."

"You don't know what you want yourself?"

"Not really, no."

Andrew wondered if the two had been lovers, although he was inclined to think they were both still quite innocent. The problem would not be quite so bewildering to the young man if his knowledge of Caroline had gone deeper than it appeared to have done.

"Just what do you want me to say to Mrs. Ramsden?" Andrew asked. "It seemed to me the other evening that she was really anxious that Caroline shouldn't stay at home to look after her."

"I rather think she is," Phillips agreed. "It's Mr. Ramsden who I'm afraid has upset the applecart. I think once he really faced the problem of how to manage without Caroline he got scared and talked her into believing it was her duty to stay. So what can I do?"

"Well, I wish I could help you," Andrew said, "but you know yourself you'll have to make up your own mind. A complete stranger like me, who knows nothing of either you or Caroline, can't possibly take it on himself to advise you."

"I think it's partly because you're a stranger that I feel I can talk to you," Phillips said. "Is that absurd?"

Suddenly it seemed to Andrew that yielding to his congenital shrinking from giving advice was in the circumstances rather pusillanimous.

"All the same, if you really want me to," he said, "I'll talk to Mrs. Ramsden and try to find out what the situation is."

"You'll really do that?" The young man's face brightened. "I'll be immensely grateful." But the brightness lasted only for a moment. "I don't suppose it'll do any good. Caroline's very stub-

born once she's made up her mind about anything. Even her
mother may not be able to make her change it."

"This job in Toronto really means a lot to you?" Andrew
asked.

"I suppose so. But perhaps it's just giving in that upsets me
most. I don't like being pushed around."

"What's your job here?"

"I'm in an accountant's office. It's not bad. I imagine I'll get
promoted sooner or later. I daresay it was just the thought of
Caroline and me going off together, leaving Knotlington, getting her away from her family, that's made it feel so humiliating
now that I seem to have failed to do that. I mean—well, it
doesn't matter. I oughtn't to be talking like this."

Andrew in his time had had plenty of the confidences of the
young, but not for some years now. He felt out of practice.

"I think you mean that you're afraid her family are more important to Caroline than you are, and of course that hurts," he
said. "But if I were you I wouldn't take it too seriously. I'd do all
I could to get her to stick to you. Don't be frightened off. It must
be possible for her mother to find help somehow, so why not
start inquiries about that? See what facilities there are for people
in her situation. There must be lots of people who are worse off
than she is, who haven't any daughter to depend on."

"Only I don't know where to begin."

"Why not talk to Mrs. Ramsden's doctor first? Do you know
who he is? See if he can give you any advice."

"Yes—yes. I might try that." Phillips' face brightened again.
"But you'll talk to her, won't you?"

"Yes, I'll see if there's anything I can do."

"And you don't think it's wrong of me to try to get Caroline
to come away with me? I mean do you think that staying here is
what she really ought to do?"

"Oh, I'm not going to discuss that. There's the alternative that
you could stay in your job here, isn't there, and it's only you and

Caroline who can decide what's the most important thing for you to do?"

"Yes, of course I see that. Well, thank you for listening to me. I know I'd no right to burden you with my problems. It was only that the Ramsdens seemed to think such a lot of you, I thought you might have some influence with them. Thank you so much. It's awfully good of you."

Swallowing his drink at a gulp, Phillips stood up. He seemed about to embark on more thanks but then in obvious embarrassment backed a few steps from the table, suddenly swung round and bolted out through the doorway to the street.

Andrew took some time to finish his drink. His coming to Knotlington for the conference, he thought, had been a complete waste of time. It might teach him in the future not to do such a foolish thing again. There had been a time when what was going forward in it would have seemed far more important to him than any of the events with which he had become involved in the last few days, but now there was something hazy about them. Feeling in his pockets for the programme of the conference, he discovered that he must have left it in his room at the hostel, and he found that he could not remember what was to happen that afternoon. So why should he not call on Alison Ramsden and get that over? It at least was something that was wanted of him. Finishing his drink, he went to one of the telephones in the lounge, looked up the Ramsdens' number and dialled it.

The ringing tone went on for so long that he nearly put the telephone down, concluding that there was no one at home. Then the ringing stopped and a voice which he thought was Alison's recited the number that he had dialled. Of course, he remembered, it would have taken her a long time, supported on her two sticks, to reach the telephone. Apparently there was no one else in the house with her.

"This is Andrew Basnett," he said. "I was wondering if I could call in on you for a little while this afternoon."

There was a slight hesitation before she answered. "Of course, I'll be delighted to see you."

"About three o'clock then?"

"Yes." She hesitated again. "Is it about something special? I mean, Gregory won't be here, if it's he you want to see."

"Actually it was you. There's something I'd like to talk over with you."

"It isn't anything to do with poor Kenneth Marriott's death, is it? Gregory's very upset about it. He's gone to the police, because there's something he thinks he ought to tell them."

"No, it's nothing to do with that."

"That's good. But it's so awful, isn't it, a thing like that happening here? The awful increase in crime in a place like Knotlington makes one feel quite frightened sometimes. Well, I'll expect you about three."

She rang off. Andrew put his telephone down and went in search of some lunch.

His taxi delivered him at the Ramsdens' flat at a few minutes after three. He rang the bell, expecting that he would have to wait for some time for the door to be opened, but after all it was not for long. Perhaps, he thought, Alison had prepared herself for his coming and had made her slow progress to the door before his arrival. Her pale face, he saw at once, showed the marks of strain. But she managed to produce a welcoming smile.

"I believe I know why you've come," she said. "One of them has been talking to you, Owen or Caroline. I suggested they should, you know. I couldn't think of anything else to do. They won't listen to me."

She turned and led the way slowly into the sitting room and to the chairs by the bay window where he had sat on his earlier visit.

"I do hope you won't think it's our fault," she said as she lowered herself carefully into one of the chairs.

"That the engagement appears to be virtually broken off,"

Andrew said as he took a chair facing hers. "I'm sure the fault isn't yours."

"It isn't Greg's either," she said quickly. "He's said that of course we can manage without Caroline. Which of them has been talking to you?"

"Owen," he answered. "And he was very anxious that I should come and talk to you about it, though I can't help feeling it's an impertinence. I'm sure I can't say anything you haven't already thought of for yourself."

"Perhaps not, but I rather hoped somehow you might have said something to them which would make them understand that it's time for them to think of their own lives, not all the time of me. I simply can't bear it that I should be responsible for ruining this chance of happiness they've got. I expect Owen will give up the idea of going to Toronto rather than really break off with Caroline, but he'll always think of it as a sacrifice he's made for her and that isn't the best basis for a marriage."

"All the same, I think it's what's most likely to happen, don't you?" Andrew said.

"I know, I know, and I'm so unhappy about it. You don't know how horrible it is being a burden on everyone, on my friends and my husband and my darling Caroline. It isn't the sort of person I am. Sometimes I think it would have been best if that car had hit me fairly and squarely and finished me off." Her voice had begun to shake, but drawing a deep breath she steadied herself. "I'm sorry, I'm not usually like this. Self-pity is one of the things one's got to learn to get over. It does one no good and it's nauseating to other people. But ever since this morning, when Caroline said she'd decided not to go to Canada with Owen, I haven't been myself."

"Owen believes it's your husband who persuaded her it's her duty to stay at home," Andrew said.

"Oh, that isn't true!" She was emphatic. "He and I had a long talk about it last night and Greg was quite sure we could manage. He's retiring soon, you know, and he'll be able to help more

at home. He even said he'd take some cooking lessons and that
we shouldn't need so very much help. Not more than we could
afford." She gave a tender little laugh. "He will too, you know.
Once he's made up his mind he's very determined."

"It sounds to me as if the person Owen should have asked me
to talk to is Caroline," Andrew said. "She seems to be the person
who's trying to upset everything. Not that I think I could do the
least good. My guess is that if they're left to themselves, the
thing will sort itself out quite satisfactorily in the end."

"But you see, there isn't much time," she said. "That's what's
so worrying. Owen accepted that job quite definitely and if he's
changing his mind about it he's got to let the people know at
once. Or at least very soon. Perhaps he can stave it off for a week
or two. He can say unexpected difficulties have arisen about his
leaving England, or something like that. But I don't *want* him to
do that. I want him to go."

"But is it really so important?" Andrew asked. "If he's a talented youngster, there'll be other opportunities."

She gave a slight shake of her head. "Of course Owen wanted
you to talk to me because he thought you might help me to put
pressure on Caroline to go with him. As if that was necessary!
But now it sounds almost as if you're taking the other side and
suggesting he might stay here."

"I suppose I was just trying to look at both sides of the question," Andrew said.

Really he did not know what side he was taking. It distressed
him to see Alison so unhappy and he would probably have said
anything that he could think of to relieve her. But it was beyond
him to guess what would actually be best for all the people
concerned. The best suggestion that had been made so far, he
felt, was that Gregory Ramsden should learn to cook and should
look after his wife himself, leaving the young couple free. But
for all Andrew knew, the man had not meant what he had said
to be taken seriously. It might have been meant half flippantly,

intended as an absurdity, almost to point up the difficulties of his and his wife's situation.

"You can get some very good frozen food nowadays," he remarked. "I often rely on it myself when I'm tired of bacon and eggs and sausages. Not that I can't do a quite good steak."

She gave him a puzzled look, not having followed his line of thought.

He explained, "I was just thinking of how you could manage if Caroline does leave you, until your husband's cooking lessons begin to bear fruit."

She responded seriously, "I see. For a moment I didn't understand . . . You live alone, don't you?"

"Yes."

"How long is it since your wife died?"

"About ten years."

"I remember her, you know. I remember you and she had me and two or three other students to tea one Sunday. She was very sweet to us."

"I'm glad you remember her."

"It's very long ago, but I do." Then abruptly she changed the subject. "I told you on the telephone, didn't I, Greg's gone to see the police about something he feels he ought to tell them about poor Kenneth. He said you advised him to do it."

"I don't think I actually did that," Andrew said. He had an impression that Gregory Ramsden had told him that it was his wife who had advised him to do it. But he could not remember for certain just what he had said in his talk with Ramsden in the library the day before. However, it was unlike him to say anything so definite.

"It was something about having seen Kenneth in the library, talking to Professor Greenslade," she said. "I don't think it can have been important, but it was on Greg's mind that he hadn't told the police about it before when they questioned him. You know, Walter Greenslade is a great friend of ours."

"You knew Marriott quite well too, did you?" Andrew asked.

"As well as anybody, I should think," she answered. "He wasn't easy to know. That image he liked to project of the fat, friendly little man, on good terms with everyone, that he liked to project, wasn't at all genuine. He was really desperately shy and very easily offended, and when he was offended he could be —well, almost vicious in a sort of way. His wife left him some years ago and I think he'd a sort of grudge against life ever after. But the motive for his murder was robbery, wasn't it? I mean, it had nothing to do with the kind of man he was."

"I don't know."

"And don't much care?" There was suddenly an edge in her voice.

"Of course I care in a way," Andrew said. "I care a little every time I hear on television someone's been murdered. Some unfortunate soldier in Ireland, or some unwary teenager on his way to the corner shop. We've got so used to horror, haven't we? And I only met Marriott once, on my first evening here. Then I may have—well, I may have almost encountered him next day in the library, but I wasn't sure at the time who it was. What I really care about most at the moment is getting home. Coming to this conference wasn't a good idea. I've been to hardly any of the sessions."

"When are you leaving?"

"Well, the affair finishes today, so I'll leave for home in the morning."

She looked thoughtfully out of the window at the small garden, momentarily withdrawn into herself. Then she looked back at him with an intently questioning glint in her eyes.

"But you think I'm right, do you, telling Caroline she should go to Canada with Owen? It's going to be hard on Greg."

"How can I possibly answer a question like that?" Andrew asked. "I don't know how much Caroline and Owen really mean to each other. I don't know what they really want themselves. My impression is that they're very much in love and that if they mess that up now it may distort them both for the rest of their lives. But I could be quite wrong and I'm not the person who'll have to pay the price for their happiness. When Owen wanted me to come and talk to you I didn't think I could help any of you much, but I didn't realise how completely helpless I would feel."

"Do you think Margaret meant it when she said she'd come and help us if we needed it? For a little while, I mean."

"Margaret?" he said, at a loss for a moment, because of his hopelessly bad memory for names, as to whom she was talking about. "Oh, Margaret Judd. Yes, I think she did."

"What do you think of her?"

"I liked her."

"She's very brave, you know. She really cared for that awful husband of hers. And would you believe it, there are still people who are sure she murdered him?"

"Mrs. Sharland, for one."

"Oh, Gwen!" Her tone was contemptuous. "Do you know she virtually lives on the money Margaret gives her? You'd think she'd have too much pride for that, but not Gwen. I believe the money means much more to her than her husband does, whatever display she makes of believing in his innocence."

It surprised Andrew a little that she should know of the payments that Margaret Judd had been making to Gwen Sharland. His impression had been that it had been an entirely confidential matter between the two women.

"Have you ever wondered if Mrs. Sharland had some hold on Mrs. Judd?" he asked.

"You can't mean blackmail!" Her tone was shocked.

"What our Superintendent Barrymore calls 'the bite,'" he said.

"Oh no!"

"Then it's a remarkable piece of generosity."

"But Margaret *is* generous."

"Then she probably meant it when she said she'd come and help you."

"Yes, I'm sure really she does—" She broke off at the sound of someone putting a key in the front door of the flat.

The door was opened and closed. A moment later Caroline came into the room. She was in the same narrow black skirt and flowered silk blouse as when he had seen her last, and had the same air of grave dignity that he had noticed then. Seeing him, she came towards him and shook his hand and said, "How do you do?" It was a greeting that he had not heard from anyone of her generation for a long time.

"You're home early," her mother said.

"I've a bad headache," Caroline said. "I asked Elfrida if I could go home. She didn't mind."

"Did you tell her why you've got a headache?" Alison asked.

"What do you mean, *why?* Headaches just come and go, don't they?"

"Oh, my dear!" Her mother gave an unhappy smile. "Why pretend with me?"

"I'm not pretending. I've got a bad headache and I want to lie down."

"You know that isn't what I mean."

A sullen expression hardened Caroline's face. "This isn't exactly the time to talk about things, is it?" She gave a swift look in Andrew's direction. "Anyway, there's nothing to talk about."

"You needn't be afraid to talk about it in front of Professor Basnett," Alison said. "He knows all about the situation. Owen's been talking to him."

"Well, I don't want to." Caroline turned towards the door. But then she paused and looked back at Andrew. "You've seen Owen?"

"Yes," he said.

"And he told you what I've decided?"

"More or less, I think."

"Then why have you been talking it over with my mother? It's nothing to do with you."

"No," he replied. "It's only that Owen asked me to do that. I suppose he thought some moral support might help her in what I believe is her feeling about the matter."

She considered that for a moment and then said uncertainly, "I'm sorry, what I said just now must have sounded awfully rude. I didn't mean it. I mean, I'm sure you thought you could help, but really there's nothing anyone can do. I can see quite clearly myself what we've got to do. The other evening I was just deluding myself. I wasn't facing facts. And I really have got an awful headache. I want some paracetamol, then I'll lie down. So you'll forgive me if I leave you and just go to my room, won't you?"

"Darling, wait a moment!" her mother said. "You've got to listen to me. You haven't thought of what it's doing to me, making me feel it's my fault you're calling off your engagement. It isn't fair to me. I haven't put any pressure on you to do that, have I?"

"No, of course you haven't." There was a note of deep weariness in Caroline's voice. "And I haven't called it off. I've only told Owen my terms. If he wants us to get married, he can stay in Knotlington. What's so awful about that? A few weeks ago, before this Toronto business came up, it was what we were thinking of doing anyhow. I'd got it all thought out. I thought we'd look for a flat somewhere near here and I could give up working for Elfrida and come round during the day and really have as much time for you as I have now."

"No!" Alison thumped the floor with one of her sticks. "If you'd seen yourself and Owen when you thought you were going away, you wouldn't come up with any suggestion like that!"

"If Owen really loves me, he'll agree to stay. But perhaps he doesn't."

"Of course he does. And I won't have it! I won't have you trying to turn yourself into a sacrificial lamb."

"But do be reasonable. How are you going to manage?" The girl's voice had become what Andrew thought of as dangerously calm, unnaturally reasonable. It might mean that an explosion

of some sort was on the way. He wished that Alison would let
her go to her room and lie down, to weep or do whatever else it
was that she wanted to do.

But Alison seemed to be working herself into a state of pain-
ful excitement and could not let the matter rest.

"If it was as simple as that, why didn't you and Owen decide
to marry until the Toronto job came along?" she cried. "The
fact is, you don't trust him now not to break the engagement off
unless you agree to go to him. I realise that. And of course that's
why you've got a headache! That's why you're so unhappy! And
it's all my fault!"

"It isn't like that," Caroline said. "If you want to know the
truth, I've told him to go and that perhaps I'll follow him when
we've worked something out here."

"You mean when I'm dead!"

"Oh, for God's sake!" the girl pleaded.

"I'm sorry, I'm sorry," Alison sank her face into her hands.
She had begun to tremble. "I shouldn't have said that. I know it
isn't what you mean. Professor Basnett, I'm so sorry to have
inflicted a scene like this on you. I know it's all my fault. We
might at least have waited till we were alone to fight the thing
out."

Taking this for a very plain statement that it was time for him
to leave, Andrew stood up. But she went on quickly, "No—
please don't go yet. I'd like you to tell me if you think I've put
any pressure on Caroline to stay here to look after me."

"No, indeed," he said.

She turned back to Caroline. "And Greg hasn't either, has
he?"

"Oh no, he's said you can easily manage," the girl answered.
"But I don't think he really knows what it means."

"Of course he does. He isn't stupid. It's all a crazy idea of your
own that you can't go. Don't you think so, Professor Basnett?"

"I can't judge how crazy it is, now can I?" he said.

She sighed, "I suppose not. But it's so detestable, having sacrifices made for one. Wouldn't you feel the same yourself?"

"I expect I should, though for all I know, I might be far more selfish than you."

Caroline suddenly went to her mother and put her arms round her. The girl laid her cheek against her mother's hair. "Let's not go on talking and talking about it," she said. Andrew saw with relief that the danger of an explosion was past. "We'll work something out. D'you know, a funny thing happened this afternoon. Gwen Sharland came into the shop and bought some flowers. She's never done that before. And she said something so peculiar. First she bought a wreath and she said it was to go on Carl Judd's grave, and then she bought some white roses and she gave a very queer sort of laugh and she said they were a peace-offering. Can you make any sense of that?"

Alison put up a hand to touch her daughter's cheek, grateful for the affectionate gesture and for the change of subject.

"It's the best flower-shop in Knotlington," she said. "All the same, it's very odd. You're sure the wreath was for Carl Judd's grave?"

"Quite sure."

"And it's the first time she's done that? I mean she didn't even do it at the time of the funeral?"

"I don't know. I wasn't working for Elfrida yet."

"No, of course you weren't. Actually I've always thought Gwen a strange sort of woman. Of course, we couldn't be friends, being as sure as we've always been that Stephen Sharland was guilty."

"That reminds me," Caroline said. "I got the impression that it was specially me she wanted to talk to. Elfrida herself could have served her, but Gwen just wandered away from her as if she wanted to look over all the flowers we'd got, then quite deliberately spoke to me. At least, it seemed to me it was deliberately. I've wondered since if she wanted me to tell you about it, but perhaps it just happened by chance."

"I expect it did," Alison said.

Andrew did not think that it had happened by chance. Gwen Sharland, whom he thought of now as an intelligent but devious woman, had wanted to send a message to her old enemies, the Ramsdens, that the war was over. Why she wanted to do this he did not know. The white roses, the peace-offering, had apparently not been meant for them. Was it possible then that they were for Margaret Judd? Had Gwen suddenly decided that after all Margaret had not murdered her husband, and had not been responsible for having Stephen convicted of murder? If she had, the murder of Marriott seemed somehow likely to have something to do with it.

Later that afternoon, after Caroline had gone out of the room to take her paracetamol and to lie down, and Andrew had said good-bye to Alison and returned to his room in the hostel, he wondered if Gwen had knowledge that Margaret could not have murdered Marriott and that, in Gwen's view, made it unlikely that she had murdered Carl. But that would mean that for some reason she believed the two murders were linked; and Andrew could not see why they should be, except that it was difficult to believe that Knotlington University was crawling with murderers. But there had been two years between the murders and the methods used in them were different. And who was to know how many more potential murderers there might be on the staff here? Andrew had never thought of academics as violent people. They seemed to work off the worst of their aggression in moderately harmless malice and back-biting. But perhaps imitation entered into the matter: One murder might stimulate more.

There was a knock at the door.

Andrew went to open it. Giles Farmoor stood there.

He looked at Andrew for a moment without speaking, and then said, "Are you alone?"

"Yes, come in," Andrew said.

He could not interpret the look on Giles's thin, thoughtful

scholar's face. It was almost scowling, as if something had made him very angry.

As he came into the room and Andrew shut the door behind him, Giles said, "We've all been fools."

"That doesn't surprise me," Andrew said. "It's what most of us are a good deal of the time. What is it now?"

"It's Greenslade," Giles said. "He's confessed to the murder of Judd."

"*Confessed?*" Andrew exclaimed. "Walter's confessed to that?"

He was deeply astonished, although not actually at the fact that Walter Greenslade should have turned out to be the murderer of Carl Judd. The thought of that had been in Andrew's mind already. But that he should have confessed to it seemed quite out of character, particularly since those two years had gone safely by without anyone seriously suspecting him of it.

"Oh yes, most fully," Giles answered with a sardonic twist to his lips. "And if he was going to do it at all, you may say, why couldn't he have done it straight away and saved that poor devil Sharland two years in hell? It took Greenslade a long time to find he couldn't live with what he'd done."

"Is he under arrest?" Andrew asked.

"Who knows? 'This fell sergeant, death, is swift in his arrest.' Too swift for my friend Barrymore. So your guess is as good as mine. I have no firm opinion about the after-life, though I'm inclined to think there isn't one."

"Giles, will you tell me what you're talking about?" Andrew said. Giles's evasiveness was beginning to irritate him. "Do you mean Walter's dead?"

"Dead as mutton," Giles answered casually. "Just waiting for the post mortem, which luckily I haven't got to do. I don't believe I could have faced cutting Walter up, even though we were never exactly friends. His housekeeper found him this morning. Stiff and cold. I only heard about it from Barrymore a short time ago and I thought you'd be interested, so I came round. Besides,

I need to talk to someone about it. I'm glad I found you. I thought you might have taken off for London already."

"How did it happen?" Andrew asked.

"He took sodium amytal, like his sister. They must have had quite a supply of it in the house for a long time. Doctors don't often prescribe it now, except for epilepsy."

"It was suicide, you mean?"

"Oh yes, didn't I make that clear? Greenslade would have never confessed and stayed alive to face the consequences. But it wasn't his conscience that caught up with him in the end and killed him. I daresay it may have been upsetting his digestion for some time. He hadn't been looking well for quite a while. It may even have kept him awake at night. I don't know about that. But it was just fear that did it at last. He was too frightened to go on living. Has it ever struck you, Andrew, that fear is the most potent of all the emotions? I used to think it was sex, the need to procreate. But I've changed my mind. Fear's even stronger than our passion for war-making and that's saying a good deal. What's kept peace in the West for an unheard-of time but the fear that, if we let ourselves indulge in the little bit of wholesale slaughter that we like so much, it'll destroy us all entirely?"

Andrew's face did not reveal the shock that he felt. It seldom did. "Giles, will you please stop making these no doubt profound remarks and come down to earth?" Andrew said. "Walter's killed himself—you've got as far as telling that. And you say he's confessed to Judd's murder. So I suppose he left a letter. Have you seen the letter?"

"Yes."

"Can you tell me what was in it?"

Giles threw himself down in a chair and began rubbing his forehead with the back of a hand. The expression on his face changed from one of a scornful kind of bitterness to one of apologetic puzzlement.

"I'm sorry, Andrew," he said. "I'm talking like a fool. It's

because I'm more than a bit scared myself. I don't know what's
happened to this place. You see, Greenslade says he'd been Marriott blackmail ever since Judd's murder. Not too much. Marriott wasn't greedy. Greenslade could afford it. But then Marriott
died, but the blackmail didn't. Someone else took over where
Marriott left off, and started asking more than Marriott had
wanted. And Greenslade didn't say who it was, or how the payments would have had to be made. But he was just too fed up to
go on putting up with that sort of thing, so he killed himself.
Disappointing for the new blackmailer, of course. No source of
income left after all, after all the trouble he'd taken."

"You mean that whoever murdered Marriott did it to take
over the blackmail from him?"

"Why else?"

"Yes, as you say, why else? It's not a bad motive. But who is
he?"

"It could have been a she, you know."

"But how and when did he or she find out that Walter murdered Judd? It can't have happened long ago, you know, or Marriott wouldn't have lived until last Wednesday."

# Eight

SINCE GILES WAS OCCUPYING the only comfortable chair in the room, Andrew sat down on the edge of the bed.

"Tell me more about this letter," he said. "It's guaranteed genuine, is it? It couldn't have been a forgery?"

"I suppose it's still got to be tested by experts," Giles answered. "But my impression, from what Barrymore said, is that there's no question about its genuineness. And if you're wondering if Greenslade's death have been murder, not suicide, I'd point out that it would have been very difficult to murder a person with an overdose of a barbiturate. It wouldn't act quickly. To get him to imbibe enough to be sure you'd kill him would be very complicated. It would have a disagreeable taste. The chances are, if you put it in his coffee or his wine or whatever he was drinking, he'd simply say, 'What the hell's the matter with this?' and spit it out."

"Where did he do it?" Andrew asked.

"Take the stuff? Up in his bedroom, apparently. He was found in his bed, with an empty bottle on the table beside him, as well as a glass with some whisky in it. But he left the letter downstairs on the desk in his study."

"How much did Walter say in his letter about Judd's murder?" Andrew asked. "Did he explain his motive? Did he say how and when he did it?"

"The motive's stared us all in the face all along," Giles said. "It was revenge for Judd having driven Veronica to suicide. That was generally discussed at the time, of course, and Greenslade hadn't an alibi. He says in his letter that he went to the Judds' house determined to kill Judd and hadn't even thought of covering up for himself, though he did know that Margaret would be out at her choir practice and that Judd would be alone. Then when he'd stabbed him, he saw the nearly finished portrait of Veronica and couldn't bear it and slashed it from top to bottom to destroy all he could of Judd's work. Then he left the house and walked straight into Marriott."

"Who was going home, wasn't he, after having had dinner with the Vice-Chancellor?"

"That's right."

"But why was it Sharland whom Marriott said he'd seen, not Walter?"

"Because he did see Sharland. First he saw Greenslade come out of the house, I imagine in an obvious state of desperate panic at what he'd done, leaving the door behind him open. So Marriott went in to see what was up and found Judd just killed and the picture slashed and the knife lying on the floor. So he appropriated the knife, realizing how useful it might turn out to be. Then he'd only just come out of the house when he saw Sharland arrive and go into it, so he waited and watched and saw Sharland come out with blood on his pullover. And later he told the police about that, but said nothing about Greenslade. And it was then, of course, that the blackmail started. And it seems to have been the conviction of the innocent Sharland that gnawed at Greenslade's conscience, so far as he had one, not the murder. There isn't a word of regret about that in the letter, but only a certain amount because of what he'd done to the Sharlands. Not a great deal, even of that, though he does say he's been near to suicide for a long time. Yet the letter somehow leaves the impression that he'd do it all over again if the occasion arose."

"But we know he didn't kill Marriott."

"No, there's no question about his alibi."

"What was Sharland's motive supposed to have been for the murder of Judd?"

Giles gave a slight shrug of his shoulders. "You don't have to prove motive, you know, though of course it helps. But the general idea that got around was that it was good old jealousy. That when Judd had got all he wanted from Veronica, he turned his attention to Gwen."

"And was there anything in that?"

"I've no idea."

Andrew had a feeling that Giles was not telling the truth. He had and idea, perhaps more than an idea, but with the evasive look that Andrew knew so well firmly in place on Giles's face, he knew that further questioning would arrive at nothing. But he remembered that on Andrew's first evening in Knotlington, Giles had asserted that Sharland was innocent.

After a moment, however, Giles went on. "There's something that Barrymore told me about, apart from the letter, that may be  significant. Yesterday was Greenslade's housekeeper's afternoon off. She told Barrymore that before she went out Greenslade had said to her that he was expecting a visitor—a woman, the housekeeper thinks, though she doesn't know for sure. Anyway, Greenslade asked her to leave the things ready for making coffee and to put some biscuits with them. The housekeeper seems to think that that indicated Greenslade's idea of a woman's taste, rather than a man's."

"Do you know of any woman in Walter's life?"

"None other than Veronica."

"Not even since she died?"

"I don't believe so, though of course I could be wrong."

"And laying on coffee and biscuits somehow doesn't sound like anything very intimate. Giles, when you said just now that Marriott could have been murdered by a woman, had you any reason for saying it?"

"Nothing specific. I just wanted to point out it was logically possible—something one shouldn't forget."

"Because I was thinking—"

But what Andrew was thinking at that moment was interrupted by a knock on the door. He went to open it.

The porter stood there.

"You're wanted on the telephone, Professor," he said. "The phone's downstairs in my lodge. The call's from a Mrs. Judd, the lady told me to tell you."

"Right, I'll come," Andrew said. But he turned for a moment to Giles. "Does Mrs. Judd know about Walter's death and confession?"

"I should think so," Giles answered. "I imagine the police will have told her by now."

"Then wait till I've taken this call. I'll be back in a few minutes."

Andrew followed the porter down the stairs and to his lodge beside the entrance to the hostel and picked up the telephone there.

"Basnett speaking," he said.

"Oh, Professor Basnett, this is Margaret Judd," the voice said. "Have you heard about Professor Greenslade?"

"Yes, Giles Farmoor's here," Andrew said. "He's just told me about what happened."

"He told you Walter Greenslade confessed to killing Carl in a suicide letter he wrote?"

"Yes."

"Ought I to feel sorry for him, do you think? I mean, to be driven to take his own life . . . I seem to feel sorry for him all of

a sudden. Then I wonder that I of all people should feel like
that. But I can't help it. But of course that isn't what I rang up
about. I don't expect it's possible but I should so much like to
see you again to talk about one or two things. Is there any
chance that you could look in here sometime this evening, or
tomorrow morning if that would be more convenient?"

"I'm going home tomorrow," Andrew said. "But I could come
this evening, say about nine o'clock."

"Any time. I'll be in all the evening and I don't mind how late
it is."

"Oh, it won't be late." Andrew had been looking forward to a
quiet evening in his room, reading one of the thrillers that his
student host had left behind him there, and then going early to
bed.

"It's very good of you," Margaret Judd said and rang off.

Andrew returned to his room, wondering what the woman
could want with him now. But the call for some reason had
made him very positively resolved that he would return to London next day.

He found Giles where he had left him.

"What did she want?" Giles asked.

"She wants me go to round and see her this evening," Andrew said. "She didn't say why."

"Probably it's just to have someone to talk to. It must have
been a fairly shattering day for her, having the past raked up in
the way it has been. And she's a lonely woman, I think. She's
been in an impossible situation for a long time, some people sure
that she murdered her husband and she herself sure of Sharland's innocence, but not knowing who the guilty person could
be. She hasn't many friends. She's really very withdrawn but
very brave."

"You seem to know her quite well."

"Not as well as I thought I did. I never knew anything about
that money she's been paying Gwen Sharland. But it's like her
to have said nothing about an act of generosity of that sort."

Something in Giles's voice made Andrew ask, "Does she mean a good deal to you, Giles?"

There was a moment of silence while Giles clasped his hands together and looked down thoughtfully at his interlaced fingers. Then he said, "You might say that—yes. A good deal."

"I've just been wondering on whose account you wanted me to come here," Andrew said. "You admitted it was something to do with your belief in Sharland's innocence, but didn't it have something to do with a desire to set Margaret's mind at rest?"

"Suppose it had, does that matter?"

It had never occurred to Andrew that Giles was capable of falling in love. His quiet life, interspersed only with a succession of corpses to be cut up, had always appeared to be sufficient for him. But perhaps, in his chosen isolation, he had somehow been drawn to someone who had had an unwanted isolation forced upon her. And yet there might be no question of his having fallen in love. It might simply be a mixture of kindliness and a sense of justice.

"Only if I'd known what I was going to be sucked into," Andrew said, "none of which is my business, I shouldn't have come. Not on your life! Anyway, no one can say Walter's death is any concern of mine. I'm going home tomorrow."

"I think that may be a good thing," Giles said gravely. "From the time you got here everything seems to have gone wrong. If I were superstitious, I'd be inclined to think that your presence has somehow precipitated things."

"Ah yes," Andrew said, "so now I'm to blame for everything. It's certainly time I got away. But Mrs. Judd isn't all that isolated, you know. The Ramsdens seem to be very good friends of hers."

"Yes, I believe they are."

"Then if she's got to talk to someone tonight, why doesn't she go to them?"

"I don't know. Perhaps she'll tell you."

"Giles, could Margaret Judd have been the woman Walter was expecting?"

Again Giles took some time before replying. Then he raised his shoulders high in a shrug.

"I'm more inclined to think it was Gwen," he said, "but anything is possible. It's possible, in fact it's quite probable, that the meeting was something professional. For instance, it might have been with one of the women who've been at the conference, or one of the staff in his department. The only thing that I can see against that is that it would have been rather peculiar for Greenslade to arrange a quiet little social or professional evening when he'd made up his mind to kill himself after it."

"Have they any idea when he did kill himself?"

"They think he died between two or three in the morning, but they haven't worked out how late he probably took the drug."

"I suppose he had made up his mind to do it before this woman's visit. It wasn't somehow a result of it."

"I don't know," Giles said again. "Your guess is as good as mine."

"But you don't think it was Margaret Judd."

Once more Giles gave a shrug. He stood up. "Well, I'll be going. I'm sorry you've got involved in all our troubles and if it's my fault, I apologize. I admit I did think you might be able to help us and that I was thinking of Margaret all the time, as well as Sharland. But I couldn't foresee that Marriott was going to be murdered, or that Greenslade would kill himself. Let's hope there aren't going to be any more disasters, or at least that you get away before they happen. I sympathize with you for wanting to get back to Robert Hooke. The long dead are such peaceful company. Good-night, Andrew."

Andrew opened the door for him, saying "Good-night."

Giles left and Andrew turned his attention to the question of where he should have dinner.

He had it presently, seated alone in the refectory downstairs.

His mind was curiously empty. He was not ready yet to cope with the thought of the death of Walter Greenslade, and not only his death but what he had confessed. The fact that Andrew had come near to thinking of Walter as the possible murderer of Carl Judd did not help in the least. He had never taken that wild guess of his seriously. He remembered too that at the time he had made it, he had assumed—to explain it—that something particular must have happened recently; otherwise, why should whoever had killed Marriott have waited two years to try to take over his blackmailing of Walter?

Someone had found out something, perhaps only in the last few days, which had made that scheme seem workable. But that man Barrymore would have thought of all that already. There was no need for Andrew to share his thoughts with him. Tomorrow he would go home and see whether or not the notes that he had taken in the library here would help him to develop something new in his approach to the life of Robert Hooke. It was far more comfortable to think of that than to ask himself why he felt so little of anything like grief at the death of an old friend, even if he was a murderer.

A taxi, for which he had telephoned from the porter's lodge, delivered him punctually at nine o'clock at Margaret Judd's house. She came to the door quickly when he rang the bell. She was in dark grey slacks and a scarlet shirt and her bright hair was tied back from her face with the usual black ribbon. She had the look of elegance and fragility and grace that was so unlike the stocky figure who appeared in all her husband's portraits.

"Thank you for coming," she said as she led Andrew into her untidy sitting-room. "There are some things I'd like to talk over with you. But would you like some coffee?"

"No, thank you," he said. "I've just had some in the hostel."

"Some brandy then?"

"If you'll have some too."

"Oh yes, I will. Do sit down. I won't be a minute."

She disappeared from the room.

Andrew sat down in a chair from which he had to remove a bundle of sewing and put it down on a stool nearby before he could sit in it. Looking idly around, disliking the great landscape or whatever it was that hung on one wall even more than he had before, he thought at first that the room was exactly as it had been when he had seen it last, and wondered what Margaret Judd did, if she ever did anything, about cleaning it. Then he suddenly saw that there was something there that certainly had not been in the room when he had been here before. It was a vase filled with very beautiful white roses. It stood on a small round Victorian table near the window. The faded velvet curtains were drawn behind it, making the flowers conspicuous. Somehow they seemed out of place, as if there were seldom flowers in this room.

Margaret returned with brandy and two glasses on a tray. She poured out brandy for Andrew and then sat down quickly on the rug in front of the fireplace as she had during his former visit, nursing her own glass in her hands.

"I don't want to talk about Professor Greenslade," she said. "That isn't why I asked you to come."

"That's fortunate," Andrew said, "because I know next to nothing about what's happened. Only what I've been told by Giles Farmoor."

"Ah, Giles," she said. "He's got a great regard for you. You're old friends, aren't you?"

"We've known each other a good many years."

"He's one of the people I'm grateful to. I don't think he ever believed for a moment I could be guilty of Carl's death."

"He's a shrewd man."

"Yes. And of course he sees a good deal of the police, his job being what it is. I think he's quite a friend of that man Barrymore."

"Has Barrymore been to see you?"

"Yes, he came this afternoon and it was he who told me about Professor Greenslade's death. And he asked me some rather odd questions. He wanted to know if I'd seen Greenslade yesterday evening."

"And had you?"

"No, I haven't seen him for ages. But he didn't tell me why he wanted to know."

"I think it's because Walter probably had a visit from a woman not long before he killed himself."

"Do the police think she'd anything to do with it?"

"I don't know."

"But I said I wasn't going to talk about all that, and here I am, doing it." She sipped a little from her glass. "I believe you went to talk to Gwen Sharland, didn't you, after I'd asked you to do that?"

"I did, yes."

"I'm very grateful. You see, I'm wondering if that had anything to do with what's happened."

"Are we talking about the flowers she brought you?"

"Yes, but how did you know that?" She looked astonished. Then she laughed. "Perhaps your nephew's right about you and you *are* a detective?"

"I'm afraid it's quite simple and not at all clever on my part," Andrew said. "I was at the Ramsdens' in the afternoon when Caroline came in. I gather she works in a flower-shop. And she told us Mrs. Sharland had been into the shop and had bought some flowers, telling her that a wreath she bought was for your husband's grave and that some white roses were for a peace-offering. And here the white roses are."

"A wreath for Carl's grave?" Margaret said, looking startled. "Gwen didn't tell me about that. How strange. D'you know, I've never put any flowers on it myself except just at the funeral, when it's a more or less automatic thing to do? And I've never visited his grave. It wouldn't mean anything to me. He isn't there."

Andrew wondered if she would have felt inclined to visit the grave if he had been there, or would that have kept her away?

Her feelings for her dead husband could hardly be anything but ambivalent.

"But Mrs. Sharland did want to make peace with you, didn't she?" he said. "She'd changed her mind about you being responsible for her husband being in prison."

"So she said when she came here," Margaret answered. "And she apologized for the way she'd treated me and said I wasn't to go on paying her money every month. She even said something about paying it back, but I shouldn't think she could do it out of her pay and I told her not to, but I got a funny feeling . . ." She paused, looking thoughtfully into her glass, then suddenly intently into Andrew's face. "D'you know, it was almost as if she felt she'd extorted that money from me as a kind of blackmail, though she'd never tried to threaten me in any way, and now she felt very ashamed of it."

"It seemed to me she thought you were paying her because you believed she had some evidence against you," Andrew said. "It seems to amuse her in a rather cruel sort of way, because she hadn't."

"But what's made her change her mind? That's what puzzles me. And I could only think it was something you said to her."

He shook his head. "It seemed to me I made no impression on her at all."

"I think you must have."

Andrew felt that there could be no harm in her thinking this, though in his own mind there was a quite different explanation of why Gwen Sharland had changed her view of Margaret Judd. But he felt no inclination to talk to her about it at the moment. She had said that she did not want to talk about Walter's death. It might be interesting, however, to discuss the matter with Gwen Sharland herself.

"Anyway, things have sorted themselves out very nicely now," Margaret said. "There's no need to talk to her about it any more, though I'm so grateful to you for having done it. You don't know what a relief to me it is that Gwen's given up this awful hatred of me. Sometimes I used to lie awake at night, almost shivering with a kind of fright because of it. Isn't that absurd? It's not as if I thought she'd do me any actual harm. But I never managed to hate her back. I'm sure it would have made things easier if I could have. I just used to puzzle how anyone could have such strong feelings about me. I'm not used to it. I don't think I've ever been a person who aroused strong feelings. Hating or loving. I don't count the funny sort of love Carl had for me. That wasn't at all passionate. He wasn't passionate about anything except his painting, though it might surprise some people to know that. It was just a kind of dependence that he had on me. That was disappointing at first as I came to understand it, but I got used to it. But there was passion in Gwen's hatred."

"I realize that," Andrew said.

For a moment, after all, he nearly told Margaret why he thought that hatred had suddenly died, but he was not quite sure enough of himself to do so. He was almost certain that Gwen Sharland must have been the woman whom Walter had been expecting on the evening before his death and that somehow during their meeting Gwen had found out that he was the murderer of Carl Judd, that her suspicion of Margaret had been totally unjust and that she urgently wanted to make peace with her.

Somehow, at least, she must have found out the truth about Walter before the afternoon, when she had gone to the flower shop to buy white roses. It was possible, of course, that she could have heard this from the police in the morning, if they had interviewed her, or even from Giles Farmoor, who knew of it. But Andrew thought that if Giles had spoken to Gwen about the matter, he would have told him about it during their talk in the hostel, and if it had not been Gwen who had been expected by Walter in the evening, who else could it have been?

What a strange thing it had been for him in any case to invite a woman to come to see him, thoughtfully arrange for her to have coffee and biscuits, presumably have some conversation with her, and then, either writing a letter confessing to a murder, or possibly having already written it, go on as soon as she left and swallow a lot of a barbiturate.

Or had he not waited until she left? Had he taken it and had she sat there, watching him slowly die?

He shook his head slightly at his own thoughts and Margaret noticed it and mistook its meaning.

"But it's true," she said. "If I hadn't met Carl when I was very young it might all have been different. I know there are things bottled up in me that might have turned me into a different kind of person if they'd ever come out. But I couldn't afford to let them come out unless I was ready to wreck our marriage. Sometimes I wonder why I wasn't. It would have solved so many things. Or perhaps not. Perhaps it's just the sort of person I am. Perhaps it would always have been the same."

"I shouldn't be too sure of that," Andrew said. "I should look around you and see if a kind of love isn't being offered to you which it might be worth your while to think about. Do think about it, anyway. Now it's really time for me to go. I'm glad to have seen you once more before I leave."

"It was very kind of you to come. I've felt so strange ever since I heard the truth about Carl's death. I suppose I've just been making use of you, talking as I have. Of course telling you that there was no more need for you to talk to Gwen was only a part of it. All the same, that's true. She and I are friends now. We needn't trouble her."

Andrew nodded and a minute or two later found himself out in the street, walking along the pavement in the light of the street lamps.

He wondered what the shortest way was from Margaret Judd's house to Gwen Sharland's flat, for he had made up his mind that before he went to sleep that night he wanted to talk once more to Gwen. What he wanted was simply to learn, if he could, for his own peace of mind, if she had been the woman whom Walter had expected the evening before; and if she had been, what had happened between them. Whether or not this would be troubling her he did not much care.

It occurred to him that no one had told him if the coffee and biscuits, ordered for this visitor, had ever been consumed. If they had been he assumed that the police knew who she was, for probably her fingerprints would have been on a coffee cup. That was something he might have asked Giles, but he had only just thought of it.

At the end of the street he found himself in one of the wide thoroughfares leading through the town, in which there were buses. Stopping a passer-by, he asked if he could tell him if there was any bus that came along it which would take him to the Botanic Garden. The man answered that a Number Seven would do it, but that the gardens would be closed at this hour. Andrew thanked him and joined the small queue that was waiting at the nearest bus stop.

He had about ten minutes to wait before a Number Seven came by. Climbing on to it, he soon discovered that he could easily have walked the distance to the gardens, for the bus had passed only three stops before he recognized the gates of the gardens and knew that he must get off there. As he remembered, he had only to cross the street and turn into the crescent where Gwen Sharland lived.

As he did this he wondered if she would open the door to him if it turned out that she was at home, or if she was the nervous sort of woman who would be too cautious to answer the ring of an unexpected visitor at this hour. It might have been wiser of him to telephone first. But since he was here he could at least ring the bell. Mounting the steps to the main doorway of the house, he pressed the lowest of the bells there, which had her name beside it, and waited.

There was no answer. But there was a light in her flat. The curtains had not been drawn over the window of what he thought was her sitting-room and the light shone out of it.

After waiting a little, he rang again. There was still no answer. He began to wonder where the nearest telephone was; then he realized that it was most improbable that a directory would have survived in the box, if there had ever been one there, and that he did not know Gwen's number. It looked to him as if the only thing for him to do was to return to the hostel and telephone from there, arranging perhaps to meet her in the morning before he left Knotlington.

But he was impatient to see her now, he could not have said quite why, except that a kind of anxiety about her possessed him. Perhaps having been told that there was no need for him to talk to her again had perversely aroused a desire to do so. After ringing for a third time without any result, he pressed the bell immediately above hers.

At first he thought that this also was going to be left unanswered, but after a moment he heard footsteps inside, pounding down the stairs and the door was opened. A boy of about twenty stood there. He wore a loose pullover, jeans and bedroom slippers. His gingery hair was tousled.

He looked puzzled at seeing Andrew and said, "Yes?"

"I must apologize for disturbing you," Andrew said, "but I wonder if you've a telephone that I might use for a moment. You see, I want to call on Mrs. Sharland but she doesn't answer the door, possibly because she's nervous of opening it as late as this to someone she isn't expecting. She isn't expecting me. But it's —well, in a way it's rather urgent that I should see her. So I thought if I could telephone and tell her who it is she might let me in."

"Perhaps she's out," the boy said.

"Only there's a light in her window," Andrew replied. "I think she must be in."

"I did see her come in a couple of hours ago," the boy admitted.

"I know it's imposing on you," Andrew went on, "but I'd be

so grateful if I could try calling her. You have a telephone, have you?"

"Oh yes."

"Then if I might try . . ."

The boy hesitated as if he wondered if there was anything sinister in Andrew's request, but then he said, "Okay, come in," and stood aside, holding the door farther open.

Andrew stepped inside and followed the boy up the stairs to the first floor. A door into one of the flats there stood open, showing that it led straight into a room that had probably once been a stately drawing-room, high and elegant. Now it contained some shabby sitting-room and dining-room furniture, a table with a typewriter on it, a television, a radio that was quietly moaning away what was probably some hit tune, and a small pink stuffed elephant lying in the middle of the floor. There was also an ironing-board at which a girl stood ironing what looked like a child's knitted sweater. She looked about the same age as the boy and was dressed almost as he was in jeans and a loose pullover.

He gestured at her and said, "My friend, Sandra."

"How do you do?" Andrew said, a greeting to which she answered, "Hallo."

He went on, "I'm afraid it's a great intrusion, but your—" He had been just about to say "husband", when he realised that that would apparently not be appropriate. He dodged the issue by saying, "I asked if I might use your telephone to see if I could call Mrs. Sharland. I very much want to see her and I'm fairly sure she's in because there's a light in her window, but she doesn't answer the bell, so it seems to me just possible she's nervous of opening the door to someone unexpected at this time of the evening. Sensible of her really. One hears of such awful things happening."

"She may be having a bath," the girl suggested without stopping her ironing. She had long fair hair, wide blue eyes and a friendly smile.

Andrew had not thought of that possibility.

"But if I might just try . . ." he said.

"Sure, go ahead." The girl nodded at where the telephone stood on a table among a heap of books and papers. Andrew wondered if one or the other of them was a student. Their child, presumably, was in bed.

"Do you happen to know her number?" he asked.

"Seven-nine-two, three-seven-six-four," the girl recited without hesitating, as if she used the number frequently rather than troubling herself to go downstairs when she wanted to speak to Gwen.

"Thank you." He picked up the telephone and dialled.

He heard it ringing in the flat downstairs and let it go on for some time before at last he put it down.

"I think she can't be in after all," he said.

"Perhaps she's one of those people who leave the lights on in their flats when they go out in the evening to warn off the prowling burglar," the boy said.

"Or she's like me, she just forgets to turn it off," the girl said. "I'm terrible that way."

"In any case, I'm very grateful to you for having let me make use of your telephone." Andrew turned to the door. "It's just that I was somehow anxious . . ."

But he did not mean to speak of his anxiety. It was not rational. It arose, he thought, merely from the fact that his desire to see Gwen Sharland and to ask her a few somewhat urgent questions had been frustrated. He was always bad at waiting to do something he wanted. But the young couple had come up with two possible and perfectly reasonable explanations of why Gwen had not answered her bell, even though there was a light in her window. It would be sensible of him to accept that.

"Thank you so much," he said.

"Our pleasure," the girl said.

But as Andrew left the flat the door was not closed behind him and he found, as he started down the stairs, that the boy

was following him. Perhaps he wanted to see Andrew safely off
the premises. Aged though he was and respectable as he was
sure he appeared, perhaps the young couple found something
suspicious in his behaviour. He went across the hall at the bottom of the stairs towards the main door of the house, and then
something made him pause.

Suddenly he went towards Gwen Sharland's door and turned
the handle. The door swung open.

It took him by surprise. He had not really expected it. Standing still in the doorway, he called out, "Mrs. Sharland."

There was no answer.

He called again and again there was no answer. Glad all at
once that he had a witness with him who would be able to state
exactly what he had done when he discovered the open door, he
said, "I think I'm going in."

"It's queer," the boy said, "I mean, leaving the light on is
pretty normal, but not locking the door if she was going
out . . ." Then he stepped past Andrew and also called out,
"Gwen!"

There was still no answer.

Andrew followed him in and went into the sitting-room
where the light was burning. It was just as he remembered it, a
neat, comfortable room with its book-lined walls and simple furniture. Nothing had altered since he had seen it last. Nothing
was out of place, though why he should think it might be he
could not have said.

"I suppose we're committing an act of trespass, or something
of the sort," he said, "but I think I'll just take a look around. Are
you coming?"

He found that he wanted to keep his witness with him.

The boy nodded, but he had begun to look worried. It was
not, Andrew thought, at the silence of the flat, left with the light
on and that unlocked door, for which there might be all kinds of
explanations, but at his determined intrusion. However, when
Andrew went into the bedroom, the boy followed him.

Here there were one or two things that might perhaps be unusual. The doors of the built-in dress-cupboard stood open. But that might be how Gwen often left it. There was also a slight rumpling of the bedspread, as if something heavy had been put down on it. That could be explained perhaps by Gwen herself having sat down on it. Andrew went on into the kitchen.

Here there were signs of a meal having been eaten and not washed up. There was a tumbler on the table beside an empty bottle of lager, and a plate on which there was a half-eaten piece of bread and butter, some left-over shreds of meat, and a knife and fork. A frugal meal, probably hastily eaten. Its being left there without having been washed up seemed to Andrew at odds with the neatness of the rest of the flat. It could mean, he supposed, that Gwen would be returning at any minute. She might perhaps just have gone out to post a letter. If that were so, it would certainly be best that she should not find him here. His motive in coming inside might be hard to explain. But he thought that he would take a quick look into the only other room in the flat, the bathroom.

At that moment he noticed that the boy was no longer with him.

Assuming that he had become nervous of possibly being caught by Gwen prowling around her flat and had gone hurriedly back upstairs, Andrew went into the bathroom. The door was open and there was no one inside. There was no doubt about it, the flat was empty.

# Nine

ANDREW NEVER THOUGHT OF HIMSELF as a particularly observant person, but he was more of one than he realised. He had only looked for a moment into the empty bathroom when his eye was caught by something that seemed to him a little strange. Not only was there nobody there, and in fact it would have been peculiar if there had been in view of the open door and the noise that he and the young man from upstairs had made going through the flat, but there was no tooth-brush either. No tooth-paste. No sponge or face flannel.

It did not mean much to him at first, but on thinking about it he returned to the bedroom and, as he now expected, he saw what he had not noticed before: there were no hairbrush or comb, no hand-mirror, no cosmetics on the dressing-table.

The rumpling of the bedspread began to mean something to him now; the heavy object that appeared to have been put down on it had probably been a suitcase. The open doors of the dress-cupboard indicated that clothes had been snatched out of it quickly and hastily packed. The light left on in the sitting-room, the unlocked door, and the snack eaten in the kitchen and not washed up all began to make sense of a kind. Haste was behind everything. Gwen Sharland had gone, had left Knotlington, had been in a great hurry to go and for all Andrew knew had no intention of returning.

But that seemed improbable. There were a number of dresses still hanging in the cupboard. Andrew was no judge of such things, but it looked to him as if they were good dresses. There was that ivory silk, for instance, in which he had seen Gwen for the first time in the staff club. He could make no guess at the kind of thing that she had taken with her, but there were several hangers with nothing on them hanging from the rail in the cupboard. Not very many. He did not think that she had taken a great deal with her. In any case, unless someone had been there to help her, she could not have taken more than would go into a suitcase that she would have been able to carry. He sighed, wishing that he had had a chance to talk to her before she went. But there was nothing that he could do here now. Leaving the light on in the sitting-room and the latch on the door as they had been when he came in, he let himself out of the flat and walked towards the main road.

He was in luck because an empty taxi came by a few minutes after he reached it. Giving the address of the hostel and climbing into the cab, he realised with a trace of shock how very tired he was. He had been aware of feeling tired earlier in the evening, but had somehow forgotten it until this moment when he slumped back on the seat and began to wonder why he had been so anxious to see Gwen. He began to feel muddled about it. A little while ago it had been quite clear to him, but now he was confused. It was a result of his tiredness, he thought, and was the sort of thing that happened to him increasingly nowadays. And no doubt it would get worse as he got even older.

Suddenly he caught himself wondering how many years he

had left. That was a question that came into his mind occasionally and he usually dismmissed it by reflecting that it was a most
useless thing to think about. He had one good friend who had
just published a very lively autobiography at the age of ninety-
three, but on the other hand a great many people died in their
seventies. He might be granted five years, ten years, even
twenty before his turn came.

Now what had he been thinking about before his mind
slipped into this groove? Of, of course, Gwen Sharland and why
he had wanted so much to see her.

Well, of course it had been because he was fairly sure that she
had gone to see Walter Greenslade on the evening before his
death, and he had wanted to ask her if he was right. He had also
wanted to ask her what had made her go to see Walter. The
coffee and biscuits put ready for her, if she had indeed been the
woman whom Walter had been expecting, made it look rather as
if he had asked her to come. And why should he have done that
unless it was to confess to her that he was the murderer of Carl
Judd and that her husband had been wrongly convicted?

No, there was something there that did not fit. The coffee and
biscuits. If you are about to confess to a woman that you are
responsible for her husband having wasted two years of his life
in prison, you do not begin by offering her coffee and biscuits. A
whisky or a brandy perhaps, of which you might yourself be in
need. All the same, Andrew was certain that Gwen had gone to
Walter's house and had either heard of his guilt from him himself, or had seen the letter that he had left behind, confessing it.

In either case, she had done nothing about it. She had waited
until the following afternoon to go to the flower-shop and buy a
wreath for the grave of Carl Judd and some white roses for her
peace-offering to Margaret. So perhaps after all he was wrong
and Gwen had not been Walter's visitor. Perhaps the other
thought that he had had about her had been right and she had
heard of his confession from the police in the morning. It was
likely that they would have spoken to her soon after Walter had

been found, to tell her that in all probability her husband would
soon be released.

And she had fled. Why?

A wave of drowsiness swamped his curiosity. It did not really
matter to him very much why any of these things had happened.
Walter, who had been a friend of sorts, was dead, as his sister
Veronica was dead, both of them beyond the reach of any kind-
ness or understanding that Andrew might have found it in himself to show them. Marriott was dead and his murderer was at
large, but that was something for the police to sort out, not a
complete stranger to the man like Andrew. He yawned and his
eyes closed. He was not quite asleep when the taxi stopped at
the hostel. Forcing himself to wake up, he paid the driver and
walked wearily to the door.

It dismayed him dismally when the porter stopped him.

"There's a gentleman waiting for you in the common room,
sir," he said. "He came at least half an hour ago, but said he'd
wait for a while in case you came in. I may have missed him if
he decided to leave, but I think he's still there. Dr. Ramsden. He
said you know him."

For a moment Andrew toyed with the idea of asking the porter not to mention to Gregory Ramsden that he had come in, so
that with luck he would eventually get tired of waiting and
would go away, if in fact he had not done so already. Andrew
could think of no reason why the librarian should want to speak
to him at this hour. But he seldom found himself capable of
treating people with even the small amount of ruthlessness that
this would have required. He thanked the porter and went on
into the common room.

Gregory Ramsden was there in the nearly empty room. He
was in one of the armchairs, apparently reading an evening
newspaper, but he must have keeping an eye on the door for he
stood up at once when Andrew appeared, and dropped the
newspaper onto a table near him.

"I'm sorry to trouble you like this at this time of the evening,"

he said, "but I'll only keep you a few minutes. I suppose we
can't get a drink in this place."

His normal briskness had left him. He looked almost as tired
as Andrew felt.

"I'm afraid not," Andrew said, dropping into one of the
chairs. "How can I help you?"

Gregory Ramsden sat down again.

"I don't even know if you can," he said. "It was just an idea of
Alison's. She said you were the most likely person to know what
had happened, because you're a friend of Farmoor's. We tried
getting in touch with him first. We tried telephoning but
couldn't get through to him, and I drove round to his place
before coming here, but he wasn't in. So Alison suggested I
should come to you, because Farmoor would probably have told
you anything he knows, and he's in touch with the police.
There've been rumours, you see, but no one I've talked to seems
to know exactly what happened. There's a paragraph about it in
the evening paper" —he gestured at the paper that he had just
tossed down—"but it doesn't say much. Just 'Professor found
dead,' and that's about all except that foul play is not suspected.
Of course they mention that it was Greenslade. Do you know
any more than that? Alison's very upset, because he was rather a
friend of hers, so I thought I'd come round to see you and find
out if you can tell me what's actually happened."

"I can tell you what Farmoor told me," Andrew answered.
"And that, I suppose, is only what the police have told him. I
think his reporting of that to me would be correct, but I can't
swear to you that I'll hand it on correctly. My memory isn't
what it used to be."

"But at least you know, I'm sure, if it's true that Greenslade
committed suicide," Ramsden said.

"Oh yes, that's true," Andrew said. " 'Foul play is not sus-
pected' —well, I believe that's true too. As I understood what
Farmoor told me, there's no possibility that he was murdered.
He killed himself in the same way as his sister Veronica did,

with an overdose of sodium amytal. I suppose there'll have to be a post mortem before they're absolutely sure that that's what he died of, but I gather there was an empty bottle of the stuff by his bed and Farmoor pointed out to me that if you wanted to murder somebody an overdose of a barbiturate would be a very uncertain way of doing it. It would be slow, for one thing, and the victim might realise that there was something wrong with him and get to a doctor in time, and also if enough of the stuff to do the job were poured into something he was going to drink, it would have made it taste foul and he'd have probably poured it away."

Ramsden nodded gravely. "Yes, I see. But why did he do it? Was he just a classic case of the manic-depressive who suddenly couldn't bear things any longer when the depressive phase was on, or had he some special reason? I can't say I ever noticed him getting very manic. Depressive—well, perhaps yes—and he'd a fairly bad temper, but I can't say I remember him ever being full of joy and excitement."

"No, he'd a quite special reason," Andrew said. He wondered how quickly he could bring this interview to a close. His tiredness was like a fog in his brain. "He left a letter behind, you see —do remember I'm only trying to quote what Giles told me— and in the letter he confessed that he'd murdered Judd because of how he'd treated Veronica. And he said in the letter that he'd been paying blackmail to Marriott for the last two years because Marriott knew he'd done it."

"And at last he couldn't stand it, so he murdered Marriott too and then killed himself? No, of course that won't do. Greenslade had an absolutely sound alibi, hadn't he, for the time Marriott was killed? I suppose that couldn't have been faked somehow. What do you think?"

"I don't think its soundness has ever been questioned," Andrew said. "Walter was speaking at a dinner of the Botanical Association about the time of the murder."

"But didn't he say anything about who murdered Marriott? Surely he had some idea about it."

"If he had, I don't believe he said anything about it in his letter."

"Isn't that strange?"

"It is rather."

"But what tipped him over at last? I mean, if he'd lived with his conscience all that time and been paying blackmail too, why did it all suddenly become too much for him?"

"I gather that when Marriott died, the blackmail didn't stop. In fact, whoever had got the knowledge of Walter's guilt from Marriott took it over and started demanding rather more than Marriott ever had, and Walter decided life wasn't worth living any longer. By the way—" he changed the subject abruptly, "—have your two young people decided anything yet? Are they going to Toronto?"

A frown of irritation, as if Andrew had interrupted some line of thought in Ramsden's mind, appeared on his forehead.

"Oh, I think that's off," he said, "and probably a good thing too. I never really believed in it myself. I saw trouble there from the start. If neither of them was ready to give up anything for the other, it didn't promise too well for the future. But Alison was very keen they should go ahead. But look, if someone after Marriott was blackmailing Greenslade, he must have known who it was. There'd have had to be some arrangement for handing over the money, and even if he'd been told to post it to some accommodation address, or something of that sort, he could easily have set about tracing who was getting it."

"I know, it's puzzling," Andrew agreed.

"Very, very puzzling." Ramsden gave a deep sigh. "Personally I feel like hell about it. I never had a particularly close sort of relationship with Greenslade myself, but he was kind to Alison. And if he murdered Judd, I'm not inclined to blame him too much. The man was asking for it, and it just happened that Veronica meant all the world to Greenslade. To me the most upsetting bit of the whole story is what happened to Sharland. I'm one of the people who was at fault there. I don't mean I ever had to give any evidence against him, but I was convinced he was guilty and didn't even think of trying to clear him. I think if enough of us had had doubts of his guilt and had done something about it, we might have got at the truth. But his motive seemed so obvious and there was Marriott's evidence and the blood-stained pullover. . . . Oh well, they'll be letting him out now, that's some consolation, though it may take some time. The law can move incredibly slowly."

"Just what was his motive supposed to have been?" Andrew asked. "Jealousy of Judd's relationship with his wife?" Andrew remembered what Giles had said on the subject. "Was that it?"

"Of course."

"You believe there was something in that?"

Ramsden turned his hands palms outwards, indicating uncertainty.

"I don't know what I believe now," he said. "I haven't questioned it all this time. I was sure Gwen and Judd had been having an affair. And that gesture of hers, coming into the staff club every evening and having her one drink and staring round defiantly, well, I thought that was an expression of guilt as much as anything. She wanted to show everyone how faithfully she was sticking to her husband. But perhaps I was wrong, as I may have been about her and Marriott."

"Marriott?" Andrew exclaimed. "You mean she was having an affair with Marriott?"

"Please!" Ramsden repeated the gesture with his hands. "I don't know what I'm saying. Don't take any notice of it. All I'm sure of is that Gwen isn't a woman who was meant to live alone. It may have been Marriott she was having an affair with, or it may have been someone else I've never even heard of. But I do think there was someone."

"I find it difficult to believe it was Marriott," Andrew said. "On my first evening here I was in the staff club having a drink with Farmoor and Marriott, and Mrs. Sharland suddenly appeared and, as you say, had her one drink and left. But before she left Marriott bolted out, as if he couldn't stand the sight of her, and Giles told me it was because it was his evidence that had convicted Sharland and he couldn't face her after that."

"A masquerade," Ramsden suggested. "Can you be sure he wasn't waiting for her outside?"

"No, of course I can't. It's just that . . ." But Andrew was not sure what it was. It might have been merely a feeling he had that Marriott had not been an attractive sort of man, whereas Gwen was a very attractive woman and could surely have found someone with more appeal, if a love affair was necessary to her. But he knew how wrong it was easy to be about that kind of assumption. The attractive are not always drawn to the attractive, who can to some extent compete with them. And Marriott might have had qualities that did not appear on the surface. He might have offered a devotion that was soothing to Gwen's pride. He might have been a very satisfactory lover.

On the other hand, there might be nothing in the idea at all. Gwen Sharland was a woman to whom gossip would naturally attach itself, but it might have no foundation whatever.

However, when Ramsden had gone, as he did a few minutes later, and Andrew had gone wearily up to his room, he found that the thought of a connection between Gwen and Marriott would not leave him. Dropping into the armchair, he leant back and closed his eyes.

But it was not to sleep yet. He had become too tense, in an exhausted, nervous way, to have any hope of that. His talk with Ramsden had upset him. That was partly because of what Ramsden had said about Gwen, about an affair that perhaps she had had with Carl Judd and another later with Marriott; but also because of his casually dropped remark that the engagement between Caroline and Owen Phillips was probably off. It was curious that that should disturb Andrew as much as it did, for he had seen hardly anything of either of them. But he remembered the glow of happiness about them both that he had seen on his first meeting with them. It had struck him even then as a rare thing, something to be fostered and treasured. If they were really going to give each other up for no very good reason it seemed a great pity.

He started thinking again of Gwen. Something about her had stayed at the back of his mind ever since his talk with Ramsden, something disturbing yet quite simple. It was merely that if she and Marriott had been intimate, she might easily have induced him to tell her the true facts about Judd's murder. And that would have meant that her daily demonstration in the staff club of her faith in her husband's innocence had indeed been a masquerade, because it had been in her power to free him at once from prison, and also that she could have picked up the blackmailing of Walter Greenslade where Marriott had dropped it. Not only could she have been the woman whom Walter had expected to visit him on the evening before his death, but it could have been her demands that had led him to take the overdose of sodium amytal.

But if that was so, why had he not named her as a blackmailer, perhaps also as the killer of Marriott, in the letter that he had left behind? Why had he not named anyone? That was really a remarkable thing. . . .

Andrew sat up with a jerk. He had been very near after all to falling asleep, and he did not want to go to sleep in the chair. It was time to get undressed and go to bed. His last waking thoughts that night were of Gwen, of her empty flat, of the open dress-cupboard, of the missing tooth-brush.

Why had she fled? Was there someone here who knew dangerously much about her? Had she attempted blackmail? Was she a murderess?

Giles had said that the killer of Marriott could be a woman and Gwen was much taller than the portly little registrar and probably at least as strong. Physically she might have been capable of the act. But emotionally . . . ?

Drowsiness won at last and Andrew fell into a deep and dreamless sleep.

He woke later than usual next morning to the sound of rain beating on the windows. Lying there, feeling more peaceful than he had during the last few days because he knew that he was going home, he reflected that it was that sound and the sight of heavy grey clouds covering the sky that brought back the Knotlington he remembered. Its climate had been about its worst feature. Nell had complained that sometimes from one end of the summer to the other she never put on a cotton dress. The fine weather of the last few days had not been characteristic of the place. And that could not be changed. Many things in the town had changed since Andrew and Nell had lived there. It was cleaner, more convenient, and altogether less dismal. But the climate had to be accepted as it was—pretty depressing.

It was odd that recognizing this was somehow cheering, bringing back to him memories of a time when he had been astonishingly happy.

He got up, put on his dressing gown, and made his way along the corridor to the bathroom for a shower and a shave. After getting dressed he nearly forgot to eat the important piece of cheese with which he normally started the day. He had his hand on the door handle before he suddenly remembered this ritual, and, going back to the dressing table where he had left the box, opened it and found to his dismay that it was empty. Of course, he recollected, he had eaten the last of the foil-wrapped triangles in it yesterday and had intended to buy some more sometime during the day. But other things had kept diverting his thoughts.

This could not be called highly important. It was not like finding himself without some drug on which his health depended. All the same, it was annoying and it was the reason why he went downstairs to the refectory in a more irritable state of mind than was usual, and why, as he finished his breakfast and the porter came to tell him that Superintendent Barrymore would like to speak to him, that he nearly snapped back that the porter should tell the bloody policeman he was not available.

Luckily he did not actually say this. If he had a moment later he would have felt very ashamed of himself. He only said that he would be with Mr. Barrymore in a few minutes, and poured himself out a third cup of coffee. The hostel coffee was just drinkable if one felt badly in need of it. Andrew deliberately took his time over drinking it, feeling that this was a way of asserting that the recent happenings in Knotlington were no concern of his, then he walked through to the common room where the porter had told him the Superintendent was waiting.

He found the Superintendent standing at one of the windows with his hands locked behind him as he gazed out at the rain. He did not turn until Andrew addressed him, then he looked round, said good morning but that it wasn't a particularly good one, was it, and that they had probably seen all they were going to see of the summer. Andrew agreed with him and led the way to two chairs in a corner of the room, since it seemed to him likely that whatever the detective had to say ought not to be overheard by the other people there, if that was avoidable. They both sat down and Andrew waited for Barrymore to begin.

He did not seem to know at first how to do so, but tugged at one of his projecting ears while his little shrewd grey eyes dwelt on Andrew's face almost as if he expected Andrew to start their conversation.

At last Barrymore said abruptly, "Of course you know that woman's gone, don't you?"

"Mrs. Sharland, do you mean?" Andrew asked.

"Yes, Mrs. Sharland."

"I supposed she'd gone," Andrew said, "but I couldn't be sure of it."

"You were round at her place yesterday evening, weren't you?"

"Yes, but how did you know that?"

"We were round there ourselves and a young couple who live in the flat over hers described a man who'd been there a little while before us, trying to get in touch with her, and who did go into the flat, and their description seemed to fit you. I'd like to know what took you to see her."

Andrew lied readily. "I wanted to congratulate her on the fact that her husband would soon be free. We'd met once or twice during the last few days and I knew how much that would mean to her."

"So you know about that, do you? About Greenslade's suicide and confession."

"Yes, Dr. Farmoor told me about it."

"Ah yes, of course you're friends." Barrymore released his ear and took to smoothing his bald forehead. "You know, I imagine, that you don't have to answer my questions, but I'd be grateful for any information you can give us. Have you any idea where Mrs. Sharland has gone?"

"None at all," Andrew said.

"Or why she went?"

"I've been trying to think that out myself, but I haven't got anywhere. Now may I ask you a question?"

"Go ahead."

"Why did you go to see her? Was it to tell her what you'd found out about her husband's innocence?"

"Oh no, we'd done that in the morning. Soon after the house-keeper had found Greenslade and had called us in and we realised it was probably suicide and his confession was genuine, one of our men was sent off to see Mrs. Sharland to tell her all about it. It seemed the decent thing to do. I mean, to let her know her husband's troubles were virtually over."

"Quite. Then why did you go to see her in the evening?"

Barrymore took to tugging at his ear again.

"It was to verify a guess," he said. "A bad one, as we've since found out."

"You thought she might be the woman whom Greenslade was expecting to visit him in the evening?"

"Oh, you know about that too. Yes, we'd been trying to find out who the woman was who came to see him and she seemed one of the possibilities."

"A woman did come to see him? You're sure of that?"

"Someone came. We knew that at once. Two coffee cups had been used and some biscuit crumbs had been left on a plate. We'd no proof till this morning that it was a woman, but the housekeeper had an impression that it was. The woman's visit might have had nothing to do with his death—in fact, it probably hadn't. I mean, if it was some colleague of his whom he felt for some reason he had to see, even though he'd practically made up his mind to put an end to things, or something of that sort. For instance, it might have been someone to whom he wanted to give a message for someone else. So we set about questioning all the women we heard about who'd had anything to do with him, and so we got around to Mrs. Sharland. But in her case there was something a bit special that made us want to talk to her. It was only a guess, as I said, but it seemed worth exploring."

"You said just now it was a bad guess."

"So we know now, but we didn't yesterday evening. You see, there was a curious thing about the letter Greenslade left behind. He didn't name the person who'd taken over the blackmail from Marriott."

"So Farmoor said. It's decidedly curious."

"There are several possible explanations, of course. One could be that he simply didn't know who it was. He could have had an anonymous letter. An unknown voice could have spoken to him on the telephone. But another possibility seemed to be that Greenslade had the remains of a conscience. There are remarks in his letter that suggest that what was really on his mind wasn't his murder of Judd, which he seems to have felt was justified— he even talks of having taken justice into his own hands—but the conviction of Sharland for something he hadn't done. And

so he could have felt, we thought, that the Sharlands had suffered enough already through what he'd done and that he
wasn't going to add the accusation of blackmail to their troubles,
particularly as he wouldn't be paying it."

"You mean you thought that Mrs. Sharland could be the
blackmailer?"

"Yes, and I still think she could, be even though she wasn't the
woman who went to see him in the evening."

"But doesn't that mean she was probably the murderer of
Marriott?"

"That thought did cross my mind."

"But you're sure now she wasn't the visitor he was expecting.
That means you know who it was."

"Yes, as it happens, we do."

"May I ask who it was?"

Barrymore gave Andrew a brooding stare, as if trying to decide how safe it would be to trust him with such a sensitive
piece of information. Then he gave a slight shrug of his shoulders, as if he had decided that it did not much matter who knew
it.

"Mrs. Ramsden," he said.

"Mrs. Ramsden?" Andrew exclaimed in bewilderment. "But
that's impossible. She's practically a cripple."

"Oh, she can manage quite a bit if she has some help," Barrymore said. "She can get in and out of a taxi all right. We found
the taxi driver who took her to Greenslade's house. That's how
we got on to the fact that Mrs. Sharland hadn't been the visitor
he was expecting. All the same, he might have had a visitor later
whom he wasn't expecting and that could—I'm not saying it
was, but it just could—have been Mrs. Sharland. So you understand we're still very anxious to talk to her."

"Have you talked to Mrs. Ramsden yet about this visit of
hers?" Andrew asked.

"No, I'll be doing that this morning."

"Your taxi driver couldn't possibly have been mistaken? I mean, it could be a case of mistaken identity."

"Oh no, he was summoned by telephone to the Ramsdens' house and helped Mrs. Ramsden in and out of the taxi and was told to wait to take her home again. It happens he's driven her before and knows her quite well."

"So the whole thing was quite out in the open."

"Yes, entirely."

"Doesn't sound criminal," Andrew said. "How long did he have to wait?"

"About twenty minutes."

"Rather a hurried coffee and biscuits then, but I suppose Greenslade wasn't feeling sociable and she may have seen it and had the tact to leave. I'm sorry I can't help you about Mrs. Sharland."

"It may be of no consequence. We'll find her sooner or later." Barrymore stood up. "But if you should hear anything about her—for instance, if she should get in touch with you—"

"There's no reason why she should do that," Andrew interrupted.

"Well, if she should, we'd be grateful if you'd let us know as soon as possible. Good morning."

Andrew said, "Good morning," and accompanied the Superintendent to the door of the hostel.

When he had gone Andrew went up to his room and packed his suitcase. This time he was not going to have second thoughts, he was going home. He summoned a taxi and presently was deposited at Knotlington's main station. He was early for the train he had decided to take, but that was usual for him. When he was catching a train or a plane, he nearly always arrived as much as half an hour earlier than was necessary in case he should find himself having to hurry anxiously to catch it. To pass the time until the train was due he bought a *Financial Times* and did his best to discover whether his modest invesments had risen or fallen. He did not really understand such matters very

well, but it was his impression today that he was a little poorer
than he had been a few weeks ago.

That ought to have been depressing, but in fact it had very
little effect on him. He had his pension, which was adequate for
him to live on comfortably, and apart from that he tended to
think of money as virtually an abstraction. Since his youth,
when he had sometimes actually gone hungry before he had
obtained his first research grant, he had always had enough. He
had never had to worry about it. So the rising and falling of the
relatively small amount that he had saved and invested was now
like a kind of game that he played, rather than anything on
which he was dependent.

But it would have been nice, he thought, as he sat on a bench
on the platform, to have something to leave his nephew. Peter
Dilly was his only living relative. Not that Peter needed anything. Since his science fiction had taken off he had become a
great deal richer than Andrew. But it would have been a gesture
of affection. Peter would have understood that, even if Andrew
himself were not around to witness him doing it. And he would
probably have recognized that Andrew would have liked him to
spend the money in one big bang, rather than hoarding it eco-
nomically. For instance, he might have bought an expensive car
or set to travel first-class round the world. Only there would
really be very little to leave him and he already had an expensive
car and if he should feel like going round the world first-class,
he could easily pay for it himself.

Peter was on Andrew's mind, however, when he approached
his home. He lived in a comfortable flat in St. John's Wood, and
as the entirely dependable woman who looked after it for him
would have been in twice while he had been away, everything,
he knew, would be well vacuumed and well polished. He found
she had even put a few roses in a vase on the mantelpiece. She
and her husband, who was a lorry-driver, had a small garden
which appeared to produce an amazing abundance of flowers
and vegetables, and she had a pleasant habit of bringing bunches

of whatever flowers were in season to Andrew. The sight of
them now made him feel most pleasingly at home.

Going out to the kitchen to fetch himself a drink, he was not
at all surprised to find a vegetable marrow on the table. Luckily
it was one of the things which he knew how to cook. He poured
out a glass of sherry and took it back to the sitting-room, sat
down in his favourite chair and kicked off his shoes. He very
seldom wore shoes when he was at home, but generally walked
about in his socks. Presently, he thought, he would look to see if
there was anything in the refrigerator that he could have for
lunch. Meanwhile, when he had drunk one glass of sherry and
helped himself to another, he began to think of Peter again.

When Peter was in England, which was not a great deal of the
time, he lived in a cottage in the village of Godlingham. The
time of year when he was most likely to be there was midsummer. In other words, he was fairly likely to be there now. Andrew took his second sherry with him, sat down in a chair by
the telephone and dialled the number of the cottage.

Peter's voice answered him, reciting the number.

"Peter?" Andrew said.

"Yes, Andrew," Peter responded. Since his infancy it had
never occurred to him to call Andrew "uncle."

"Peter, what have you been up to," Andrew said, "telling
Margaret Judd that I've a habit of solving murders?"

"Well, haven't you?" Peter said.

"No," Andrew said. "It's only been by pure chance that I've
ever got involved. But this time it wasn't chance, it was your
doing."

"I don't think I know what you're talking about," Peter said
apologetically.

"You haven't read anything in the newspapers about the murder in Knotlington?" Andrew asked.

"No—oh yes, but not in the papers. There was a mention on
television. Don't tell me you've been in Knotlington."

"Yes, and I went there in all innocence to a scientific conference. And what do I find? I find a woman you know who was told by you that I'm a great detective, a woman whose husband happened to have been murdered a couple of years ago, and she's talked to a man who's a very good friend of mine, Giles Farmoor—you've probably heard me talk about him—and he'd written to me, urging me to come to the conference. If he hadn't done that, I don't suppose I'd have gone. I'm past that sort of thing. But as if that mattered! I had hardly any chance to attend any of the sessions, because Giles and this woman and one or two other people seemed to assume I'd arrived there to solve one or two murders for them. Now I'm at home again, thank God, leaving these problems in the hands of a very competent policeman whose job it is to solve them. And I'm telephoning while my feelings on the subject are still hot to ask you never again to spread around the story that murders are my hobby."

"Well, aren't they?" Peter said.

"Please be serious."

There was silence at the other end of the line. Then Peter said, "And you didn't solve anything?"

"Nothing at all."

"You know, if I were you I should think again," Peter said. "The chances are, I believe, that you've got something tucked away at the back of your mind which might help the police, even if it doesn't clear the whole thing up for them. Exactly who was it who got murdered this time?"

"Exactly," Andrew said, "a man called Marriott. Registrar of the University. Someone knocked him out by bashing him on the head with a bottle, then cold-bloodedly strangled him."

"But why?"

"Oh, it's a long story."

"Go ahead."

"Well, it seems he'd been blackmailing the man who'd actually murdered Carl Judd and who committed suicide a couple of nights ago, leaving a letter behind confessing what he'd done. Walter Greenslade. You may have heard me talk about him too."

"I think I have. Wasn't he once a student of yours who did rather well? So he murdered this man Marriott, then killed himself?"

"No, no, nothing of the sort. Walter had an impeccable alibi. He was making a speech at the dinner of the Botanical Association about the time Marriott was killed. No, whoever killed Marriott probably did it to take over the blackmailing of Walter from him. That, at least, seems the likeliest motive."

"And Greenslade thwarted him by killing himself. What bad luck for whoever it was, when he'd waited such a long time to get around to doing it. Why do you think he waited all that time since Judd's murder?"

"I suppose because it was only recently he found out the truth."

"You keep saying 'he.' Couldn't it have been a woman?"

"It could have been, yes."

"What will you bet that it was a woman?"

"Nothing at all, thank you."

"You don't believe it?"

"I've no opinion on the matter."

"Oh come, Andrew, you must have at least an opinion, even if it's wrong. You've had some days to brood about it. You must have an itchy sort of feeling in your fingertips, or wherever it is that you get itchy feelings, that you know more than you're letting on. And however glad you are to be home, you know, you won't be content till you've got the thing sorted out. Try thinking about all the really unimportant things that happened since you got to Knotlington and see if you don't come up with something."

A feeling that there was something in what Peter said, indeed a good deal, perhaps that he was absolutely right, caused a mood of intense irritation in Andrew.

"I didn't ring you up to go into all this," he said. "I did it merely to request that you never in any circumstances repeat what you've done. Do not tell any of your friends that I'm a specialist in murder. Do not, I repeat, do *not* get me involved again in the sort of thing I have been involved with in Knotlington."

He was not sure but he thought he heard a chuckle on the line.

"I'll promise to do my best," Peter said. "Very few of my friends have had their husbands murdered, so you may be safe. Anyway, it was nice to hear from you. Now sit down quietly and think. I've the utmost faith that you'll arrive at something. Good-bye."

"Good-bye."

Andrew put down the telephone and went to see what was in the refrigerator.

There was some cold ham and some bread which, when it was thawed out, could be made into tolerable sandwiches. Assembling them with butter and mustard on a tray, he carried it to the sitting-room, nearly tripping over the shoes which he had kicked off and in a way that he had, and left in the middle of the room.

He was no longer irritated by Peter's advice that he should sit quietly and think. It was what he would probably have done in any case. But his thinking was not about what had happened in Knotlington, except insofar as it was connected with what he had read in the library in the diary of Robert Hooke's amorous female relative. It was pleasurable to think about that and to consider how he could weave what he had read into what he had already written. A certain amount of that would of course have to be scrapped, but he was used to doing that and at times even enjoyed the bold crossing out of paragraphs of careful writing which it had cost him much thought to compose in the first place.

In the meantime, when he had finished his lunch, it seemed a pleasant idea to lie down and have a sleep. He had had no chance to do this while he had been away and in fact it was not a thing that he often did. But today the prospect seemed attractive. After carrying the tray back to the kitchen and washing up the plate and the knife that he had used, he went to his bedroom, lay down and expected to fall asleep in a few minutes.

In fact, he stayed wide awake. He could not stop thinking about Robert Hooke. This trying to write his life was of course all nonsense. It was time he faced that and gave up. But how would he spend his time if he did that? Perhaps, after all, there was no need to give it up, but only to change his approach to it. If he could bring himself to think that it was publication that counted, and that what he had already written would be adequate for this if he shaped it up a little, he might get it off his mind. And then he might start on something else—a life of Malpighi, that noted plant anatomist, for instance. It might make a stimulating change. All the same, there was something about Robert Hooke nagging at his mind today, and after stirring restlessly on his bed for a while he gave up the attempt to sleep, got up, went to his desk and started poring over the notes that he had made in Knotlington.

He decided to go out for dinner that evening, since there was next to nothing to eat in the flat, and he went out early to a small restaurant in the Finchley Road where he often went when he could not be bothered to cook for himself. Returning after he had eaten, he found that there was a film on television which he thought he could bear to watch, and after kicking off his shoes again he settled down in front of it to spend a quiet evening. He went early to bed and this time fell asleep almost as soon as he lay down.

He woke much later than usual to the sound of rain beating on the windows. So it was not only in Knotlington that rain could pour down in mid-July. London could equal it. He got up, had his usual shower and shave, and only at that point remembered that his cheese was finished and that as today was Sunday he would not be able to buy any more. So he must survive without it.

Perhaps that would be good for him. At his age there might be some virtue in not allowing himself to be gripped too firmly by habit. There was one other habit that he wished he could break, and that was the reciting of bad verse to himself. While he was dressing some words took possession of his mind:

> *There is a Reaper, who's name is Death,*
> *And, with his sickle keen,*
> *He reaps the bearded grain at a breath,*
> *And the flowers that grow between . . .*

"Who's name is Death?" Yes, that was the question, whose? But spelled as it just had been in his imagination, it was of course a misquotation. Interesting, though, that that was how he had thought of it.

The front door bell rang.

It interrupted Longfellow effectively, and as Andrew, who assumed it was the postman until he remembered that it was Sunday, was by then dressed in shirt, trousers, and socks, he went immediately to answer it.

Gwen Sharland stood there.

"I know it's very early to call," she said, "but may I come in and talk to you?"

# Ten

WITH GREAT EMBARRASSMENT, Andrew was aware that he had not combed his hair and was wearing no slippers.

"Yes, yes, of course, please come in," he said, stepping back so that she could enter. "I was just going to get breakfast. You'll have some, won't you?"

"Coffee?" she said. "Are you going to make coffee? I'd love some."

"Nothing else?"

"No, thank you. I've had all the breakfast I can eat."

She gave the impression, though Andrew could not have said quite how, of having been up for some hours. There had been time for her strange green eyes to grow tired. But perhaps all that meant was that she had not slept much. She was in a dark blue suit with the jade brooch that he remembered on her lapel. She moved with an air of weariness.

He took her into the living room, but as soon as he had done that he saw that the shoes he had kicked off the evening before were still lying in the middle of the carpet. He picked them up hurriedly, told her to sit down and that it would take him only a few minutes to make the coffee, and darted back into his bedroom, where he combed his hair and put on a cardigan and slippers; then he went into the kitchen and poured beans into the coffee-grinder. When presently he emerged with a tray on which there was coffee for them both, and toast and marmalade for himself, he found her not sitting down but prowling round his bookshelves, studying what he kept there.

Turning towards him as he came in, she said, "They tell me you're writing a book."

"Yes—well, yes and no," he said. "Who told you?"

"I forget," she said. "Does it matter?"

"No, of course not." He still felt flustered by her unexpected arrival. "Only I'm thinking of giving it up. I can't see it ever getting published. Milk and sugar?"

"Just black, please." She sat down at the table on which he had put the tray. "I suppose you think it's unforgivable of me, walking in at this hour."

"Not in the least, just puzzling." He sat down too and poured out two cups of coffee, picked up a piece of toast and spread butter and marmalade on it. "I tried to call on you the other evening, but you seemed to have gone. But you'd left a light on in your sitting-room and the door to the flat unlocked. That was puzzling too."

"I really did that?" she said. "Of course I was in a hurry, I suppose that's why I did it. But I'm often careless about things like that. Why did you try to call on me?"

"Suppose you tell me first why you were in such a hurry to leave," he said, "and why you've called on me now."

"I was in a hurry to leave simply because I'd a train to catch," she answered. "It was the last London train that evening and I hadn't really allowed enough time to get to the station. I did catch it by the skin of my teeth, and I'd only just got on to it

when I realized what an absurd thing I was doing. I mean, today
being Sunday. But I was in such a state of excitement that I'd
simply forgotten about that, and now I'm in London it seems to
me I might as well stay till Monday and I've today to fill in, and
that's partly why I came here, though of course I very much
want to talk to you too."

"Would you mind telling me why you wanted so much to get
to London," Andrew said, "and why it matters, today being
Sunday?"

"Because everything's closed, of course. People's offices.
Though I suppose they'd have been closed on Saturday too. People like solicitors don't work on a Saturday, do they?"

"Not many of them, I imagine, unless there's some special
reason for it. So you came to London to see a solicitor."

"Mainly." She had her elbows on the table and was nursing
her cup of coffee in both hands. "You know about Professor
Greenslade's death and his confession, don't you?"

Andrew nodded.

"Well, it means that Stephen will be released from prison
soon, of course, and I wanted to see our solicitor here in London
—my family's solicitor, I mean—instead of the man who han-
dled our affairs in Knotlington and made such a mess of everything. I know how slowly things can move, and I wanted this
other man, who always used to be very efficient, to take the
matter in hand and see that Stephen's let out as soon as possible.
Now that we *know* he's going to be let out, it must feel absolutely intolerable, being kept shut up."

"I can understand that. But does he know yet about Walter
Greenslade's confession?"

"I don't know. I don't know anything. I went into a sort of
state of shock, when the police had been to see me and told me
about that confession, and now I hardly know what I did. I got
some flowers and took them to Margaret because I realized how
horribly unjust I'd been to her and how good she'd been to me,
and I sent—I think I sent—some flowers to be put on Carl's

grave. A ridiculous thing to do, but I really wasn't quite responsible for my actions. You see, I'd always believed—well, half-
believed—no, I won't go into that."

Her eyes looked into Andrew's in a long, questioning stare, as
if she were wondering how much sense he was making of what
she was saying.

He reached for a second piece of toast and spread it with more
butter and marmalade.

"You half-believed your husband was guilty of Judd's murder," he said. "Hence your slightly over-dramatized display of
your belief in his innocence every evening in the staff club."

"That was what you thought it was, did you?" she said.
"Over-dramatized."

"Somewhat."

"I never thought anyone could think that, but perhaps you're
right. But you don't know what it cost me to do it. I had to do
*something*, I felt, because I was so much to blame."

"Because of your affair with Judd?"

"Oh, you know about that too, do you?"

"I've heard gossip, but really I'm afraid I was just guessing."
She put down her cup, nodding thoughtfully over it.

"You were quite right. Yes, we'd had a affair of sorts, after
he'd broken off with Veronica. And Stephen got to know about
it and he wasn't exactly jealous—that isn't the right word for it
—but he was terribly hurt, though he didn't try to interfere, and
he used to mutter that he'd probably kill Carl if he was a different sort of person, and that he might kill me too if he could
think of a way of getting away with it, and then he'd laugh and
he might even kiss me and say he hoped I was happy at last.
Which I wasn't, I was miserable. I felt rotten to the core, because Stephen was so good and generous."

"But you're dead scared of what may happen when he comes
out of gaol," Andrew said. "That's really why you want to see
your solicitor, isn't it? You probably want to talk about divorce."

She frowned in an absent way, almost as if she had not heard what he said, but then replied, "You're good at guessing."

"But if you thought all along your husband might be guilty of Judd's murder," Andrew said, "you must have also thought all along that Margaret Judd was innocent."

"Of course."

"Yet you took the money."

"Oh yes."

"Why?"

"Because I needed it. My work brought in very little. And it amused me in a way to pretend I was blackmailing her. Sordid, I expect you think, but it seemed to justify taking the money in a way, because I wasn't absolutely sure Stephen had murdered Carl and I thought just perhaps she'd done it, in which case she deserved to pay."

"Have you ever blackmailed anybody else?"

She frowned again. "What do you mean?"

"Just what I asked you. Have you?"

"No, certainly not."

"Or even tried to?"

"I don't understand," she said. "Why are you asking me this?"

"Let me ask you something else. Did you visit Walter Green-slade the evening before his death?"

She pushed her cup towards him. "May I have some more coffee? No, I can't remember when I saw him last."

Andrew refilled her cup. "Someone did, you see. Someone, who may have murdered Marriott and who also got the information out of him, probably called on Walter late that evening and told him he knew he'd murdered Judd, and demanded money. And that was just one thing too many for Walter, who'd been near a breakdown for some time—anyone could see that—and so he killed himself."

"And you've been wondering if that was me."

"I have," he admitted.

She looked oddly as if the thought of it pleased her, but drank some coffee before replying. Then, with a faint smile, she said, "How simple everything would be if that were true. You've been wondering if I could have murdered Ken Marriott."

"That among other things."

"For instance, if I'd been having an affair with him."

"You said I was good at guessing, but you aren't bad at it yourself."

"You really thought that?" She was still smiling. It was more completely a denial than anything that she could have said would have been. She made it seem merely ridiculous.

"All right, I was wrong," he said. "I think you're a person it's easy to be wrong about. I shouldn't be surprised if you're often wrong about yourself."

"That's perfectly true. I often think I'm a horrible person. Then I think I'm no worse than most people. And which is right? I simply don't know. But truly I didn't try to blackmail Professor Greenslade."

"I believe you," he said, not completely certain if he meant it. "And that affair with Marriott?"

"It never happened. He never appealed to me in the least, and I don't think I did to him."

"Would you care to hazard a guess as to who could have killed him?"

She shook her head. "Wasn't his place rifled after he was killed? Wasn't it probably a common or garden burglar whom he disturbed?"

"It could have been."

"But you don't think so."

"No. But don't let's go on with that. Neither of us seems to know enough to arrive at anything. And you still haven't told me why you came here this morning."

She sighed, leaning back in her chair and letting her gaze wander around the room as if she were wondering for the first time what had brought her there. Then her eyes met Andrew's

again, this time with more expression in them than before, an
expression of faint bewilderment.

"The trouble is, you aren't really the person I took you for,"
she said. "I thought you'd be easy to talk to, but you aren't. All
these questions you've been asking me, I wasn't prepared for
them. They've muddled me up. I thought I was just going to tell
you how I'd suspected Stephen of killing Carl, and how I
thought that was my fault and that was my I'd made a big thing
of believing in his innocence, and I wanted to ask your advice
about what I should do when Stephen came out. He knows I've
suspected him, you know. I could tell that from the way he's
looked at me and wouldn't talk when I've been to visit him. So I
wanted to know, did you think he could ever want to live with
me again, or should I just quietly disappear—go abroad, perhaps, and get a job teaching English somewhere, or something
like that. Or would that be too cowardly? You see, I'd reached a
stage when I absolutely had to talk to somebody. I'd too much
on my conscience. D'you know, I spent most of last night wondering if I should kill myself, just as Greenslade did? I'd some
sleeping-pills with me, enough to do the job, I thought. And I
thought I'd leave a letter behind in which I confessed to having
tried to blackmail him and driven him to his death, because I'd a
sort of feeling that whoever did it deserved to get away with it.
Do you understand what I'm trying to say?"

"I think so," Andrew said, "only I don't believe it."

"You mean you don't believe I thought of killing myself?"

"Oh, haven't we all done that at some time or other in our
lives? I know I kept thinking about it for some time after my
wife died. But that was all I did—think about it—I never actually reached for the bottle of pills. No, I mean I think you came
to see me to try to find out something, not to tell me anything. I
think you did go to Walter's home late in the evening to try to
blackmail him, and you got in, I don't quite know how, but I
suppose his front door must have been unlocked, and you went
looking for him in his study, but all you found there was his

letter which told you the truth about Judd's murder. So you knew all about it already when the police told you about it in the morning, but naturally you didn't want them to know that, so you did that act of yours, buying the flowers for Margaret and the wreath for Judd's grave, over-dramatizing the situation in that way you have. And you came here to see if you could find out how much of this is known to the police now. You know of my friendship with Giles Farmoor and of his connection with the police. There was a good chance that I could tell you what you wanted to know. As I have. To the best of my knowledge, the police don't yet know anything of your visit to Walter."

She stood up swiftly, putting her fists on the table and leaning on them, and hissed into his face, "Are you saying I murdered Marriott?"

"As a matter of fact, no," Andrew said. "There could have been someone else. I've wondered from time to time if there might not be more than one person involved in this, and I'm inclined to think it was probably a man who did the killing."

"But you think I know who it was!"

"That wouldn't surprise me."

"You're wrong, you're altogether wrong, I never went near Greenslade's house that evening, and I didn't know of his confession till the police told me about it next day, and buying the flowers wasn't over-dramatizing anything, I bought them just because I wanted to make a—a gesture, but not a dramatic one. And I came to see you just for the reason I told you, but I wish to God I hadn't."

She crossed the room rapidly, and a moment later Andrew heard his front door slam behind her.

He poured out some more coffee. His problem was that he believed her. Trying out his theory on her of how she might have been involved in Walter Greenslade's suicide, he had been aware of a certain big hole in it. It was that unlocked front door of Walter's. If you are about to kill yourself is it not a normal kind of precaution to make sure that no one is going to be able to wander in and find you and perhaps call ambulances, doctors, police, and bring you back unwillingly to life? You would probably be particularly careful about it if you had left behind, in a conspicuous place, a letter confessing to a murder. And though it had been Walter's housekeeper's afternoon off, and she might have been out when he took the fatal overdose, she presumably had a key with which she would have been able to let herself in when she returned and she would not have gone into his study or his bedroom before going up to her own. So that upset most of his case against Gwen Sharland. She would not have been able to get into the house unless Walter himself had let her in.

What did he think about that? Andrew sat for longer than usual over his breakfast, though he had had all the coffee he wanted. In the circumstances, he thought, he had not been kind to Gwen Sharland, who might have come to him simply for the reason that she had given him. He rather regretted it, yet he wished that he had the opportunity now to be unkind in the same way to several other people, because it might help him to clear his mind. But a disturbing thing about her visit was that it had upset his comfortable feeling that all the events that had happened in Knotlington were no concern of his. When he had washed up the breakfast things and settled down at his desk with his notes on Robert Hooke, he found that he could not concentrate because a picture of the dead Walter floated before his eyes, along with a much uglier one of the little registrar, horribly strangled, and one of Carl Judd, dead so long ago, stabbed and bloody. Robert Hooke seemed very remote.

Yet the thought of him was curiously insistent. There was something about him that Andrew had never realized before and it felt important to discover what it was. Only he did not seem to be in the mood to do it this morning. He struggled on for a time, then gave it up and soon after eleven o'clock poured out his first glass of sherry.

Sitting down in his favourite chair, he put the glass on the low table beside him, folded his hands on his stomach and gazed up at the ceiling. He thought of the advice that his nephew Peter had given him. Peter had told him to think about all the really unimportant things that had happened since he had arrived in Knotlington. Of course all kinds of unimportant things had happened and it would be useless to try to catalogue them. There had been meals in the hostel. He had taken taxis. He had walked in the Botanic Garden. He had had drinks in the staff club. He had worked in the library. . . .

He drank his sherry, then poured out a second glass as a sudden feeling of excitement came to him. But at the same time he thought regretfully that he would have to go out for lunch, unless he could face opening a tin of baked beans which he had noticed in the store cupboard in the kitchen.

No, he thought, not baked beans. He would go out. But first there was a telephone call that he would make. He looked up the number in the notebook that he kept beside the telephone, dialled the number and when the telephone at the other end of the line was lifted, said, "Giles? This is Andrew."

"In London, are you?" Giles Farmoor asked.

"Yes, I'm at home. But I'm just thinking of coming back to Knotlington. I'd like to talk to you."

"Come and stay with me then. I've a reasonable spare room."

"May I do that? Thank you."

"When will you be arriving?"

"I don't know. I haven't investigated the Sunday trains. The service on Sundays always used to be terrible."

"It still is."

"I suppose I'll get there sometime in the afternoon."

"I'd meet you if you'd let me know when you'll get here."

"Don't bother about that. I'll take a taxi. But meantime, Giles, can you tell me something? When Walter's housekeeper came home after her afternoon off, did she find his front door locked or unlocked?"

"I don't know, but I can probably find out from Barrymore

before you get here. Why, Andrew? Have you any special idea about it?"

"I'm not sure."

"Is it the reason why you're coming back?"

"It's part of it. But can you find out something else for me? Owen Phillips's phone number."

"Phillips's? Why is he on your mind?"

"I want to see him, that's all."

"If he isn't in the phone book, as he probably isn't, because I think he lives in lodgings, I can get the number from Caroline Ramsden. Do you want to see her too?"

"No, no, it's just Phillips I want to see. Well, thank you for putting me up, Giles. It's very good of you. I'll be along presently."

He put down the telephone.

After a moment he picked it up again and dialled Timetable Enquiries at Euston. He was told that there was only one train to Knotlington before the late afternoon, and he realized that to catch it he would have to hurry. Bundling a few things back into the suitcase that he had only half-unpacked the day before, he walked out into the Finchley Road, went to a taxi-rank nearby where he was fortunate enough to find a taxi waiting, and hating the feeling of having to hurry to catch a train and being almost certain that he was bound to miss it, in fact caught it with just seven minutes to spare. As he did so he thought that this at least solved the problem of where he should have lunch, since he could have it in the restaurant car.

But once he had had lunch and was settled in a seat in an almost empty carriage, he began to wonder how he could have acted so precipitately. For a little while in the morning, while he had been drinking his sherry, it had seemed to him that he had grasped something of vital importance, and that it was his duty to return to Knotlington to make sure that his understanding of the matter was imparted to Superintendent Barrymore. Only wasn't it probable that the man had thought of it himself? Andrew was seldom inclined to assume that he was cleverer than other people. It was true that he had certain information that no one but himself could have obtained, but then Barrymore might have information that was denied to Andrew. He began to feel a fool, reflecting that he would be compelled to make his ideas sound reasonable to Giles, as they would be seeing each other soon, but that he was not sure if he could do it. The whole thing could be a mare's nest.

The train as usual gave its little hiccup opposite the great grey cylinders of the gasworks just before reaching Knotlington. It remained there for about three minutes, then ambled on slowly into the station. Andrew was not altogether surprised to find Giles waiting for him on the platform. He could easily have guessed on what train Andrew was likely to arrive, since the next one would not have got in till the evening. What did surprise Andrew was that Giles had Margaret Judd with him. Andrew caught sight of her mane of bright hair before he had even seen Giles.

He and Margaret advanced to meet Andrew, both looking self-conscious.

"Margaret was with me when you telephoned," Giles explained, "and was anxious to see you if you were coming back."

"I hope you don't mind," Margaret said.

Andrew did mind. He had expected to find it difficult enough to tell Giles why he had returned, but at least had assumed that he could do this in privacy. If an audience were to be forced upon him it would be twice as difficult.

"No, no, of course not," he said insincerely and tried to look as if he felt very pleased to see Giles and Margaret together.

"I've got Phillips's number for you," Giles said, "and he said he'll stay in all the afternoon since you want to get him. But I think he's got Caroline with him."

"That's quite all right," Andrew said, though again he was not sure that it was. He had not thought out at all clearly how he wanted to handle the matter.

"My car's outside," Giles said. "And about that other thing you wanted to know, whether Greenslade's door was locked when his housekeeper came home—yes, it was, so Barrymore told me. He'd thought about that himself and questioned her. She's quite certain it was locked as usual and that she had to use her key to let herself in. So if anyone called on Greenslade after Alison Ramsden left, he must have let him in himself."

"I see. Thanks," Andrew said.

They made their way out through the booking hall to the car park and to Giles's car. Andrew was feeling increasingly troubled. It had not occurred to him that there might be any difficulty in arranging to see Owen Phillips alone, and the more he thought about it during the short drive to Giles's flat, the more clearly he recognized that of all the people who might have been with Phillips the one who would be most troublesome was Caroline. Not because of anything that she might say or do herself, but simply because of the limitations that her presence would put on what Andrew intended to say. He told himself that he would have to proceed very carefully.

When they arrived at the flat Giles wanted to make tea, but Andrew said that if he didn't mind, he would like to telephone Owen first. Giles gave him the telephone number he wanted, and then he and Margaret tactfully withdrew to the kitchen to make the tea, leaving Andrew alone in the living room to make the call in private.

Whoever answered was neither Owen nor Caroline. It was a man who sounded irritated when he heard it was Owen Phillips who was wanted, as if he had been expecting a call himself and was put out that this one was not for him. Andrew presumed that this was one of the other lodgers who lived in the house where Owen had a room. The man told Andrew to hold on and that he would fetch Phillips. A minute or two passed, then Owen's voice announced that he was there.

"This is Andrew Basnett," Andrew said. "I very much want to talk to you, Owen. Can I see you?"

"What, now?" Owen said.

"The sooner the better."

"I see. Well, yes. Yes, of course." Owen seemed to be thinking it over. "It's important, is it?"

"I think so."

"Because I've got Caroline with me, but I don't suppose you'd mind if she comes along. Where shall we meet?"

"As a matter of fact, I'd sooner see you alone," Andrew said, hoping that that was not going to give offence. "It's a rather confidential matter."

"I see," the young man said, though it did not sound as if he did. "All right, I'll come on my own."

"Then suppose we make it the Royal Midland in about half an hour." The Royal Midland was the largest hotel in Knotlington, one of the roomy railway hotels of the past where it would be easy to talk privately in the big lounge. "No, make it an hour." Andrew had just remembered that tea was being made in the kitchen and that if he were to walk straight out of the flat immediately on arriving, ignoring tea, then Giles might reasonably take umbrage. And what did a delay of half an hour matter in what he had to say to Owen Phillips? What would it matter if the meeting was put off till the following day? It was mostly Andrew's own peace of mind that was concerning him, he realized. Having driven himself against the grain to take action, the sooner he could get on with it the better.

Margaret came into the living-room, carrying a tea tray and with Giles following her. It seemed to Andrew that she had an air of belonging there and he more than half-expected to be told at any minute that she and Giles had decided to get married. But if they had they were keeping it to themselves for the moment. Margaret poured out the tea and Andrew told them of the arrangement that he had made to meet Owen at the Royal Midland.

"I'll drive you there," Giles said, "and pick you up if you know when you'll want that."

"I'll walk," Andrew said. "It isn't far."

"I don't want to seem curious," Giles said, "but I suppose this is somehow connected with Greenslade's death and the mysterious blackmailer who drove him to it."

Andrew glanced at his watch. "There isn't much time to talk about it now, but I'll tell you all about it when I get back. The truth is, I believe I can explain it all, but I want this talk with Owen first because there's something I want to prevent, if I can. Something that would be rather dreadful."

Giles gave him one of his long stares, then nodded slightly, showing that he recognized that he was not the only person who did not always share all that was in his mind with others.

In spite of Andrew's protests that he could walk to the hotel, Giles drove him there, leaving him on the steps of its still soot-blackened, stately entrance. Andrew went into the lofty lounge with its great chandeliers, its mirror-covered walls, its exuberantly patterned carpet, and its small round tables spaced comfortably far apart, surrounded by low chairs and sofas. Owen was there already and stood up as Andrew went towards him. But as Andrew had feared might be the case, he was not alone. Sitting in a corner of one of the sofas was Caroline.

She looked up at him with a frown and said abruptly, "Why didn't you want me to come?"

"Shall we have some tea?" Andrew said. After the tea he had just had he did not in the least want any, but it was early for a drink and he felt that he ought to offer them something.

"Why didn't you want me to come?" she repeated.

"Well, it was just that . . ." He paused, having no idea how to answer her. The one thing that he did not intend to do was to tell her the truth. Not the whole truth, anyway. "It was just that Owen and I had a talk the other day when he seemed to want my advice, and I wouldn't give him any. A complete stranger like myself, I thought, how can I possibly tell him what to do? But I've been thinking it over since and I thought I might be able to help a bit after all. At least I ought to try. And I only wanted to talk to him alone because of our having talked alone before and because I thought he might prefer it. But if that isn't so, of course there's no reason at all why you shouldn't have come. Perhaps after all it'll be best."

"It's something to do with his going to Toronto, isn't it?" she said.

Owen put out a hand quickly and covered one of hers with it. "Let's not go into that now."

"But it's what he wants to talk to you about," she insisted. "What else could it be?"

Owen turned back to Andrew. "Is that it?"

"Yes, I've been hoping that you've decided to go," he said. "Have you come to any decision yet? And what about some tea?"

"For God's sake, forget the tea," Caroline exploded. "Why should he go to Toronto? And what's it got to do with you?"

"Nothing at all, I'm afraid," Andrew answered, "but I can't help feeling you'll regret it if you don't go. From what I understood of it, it sounded a great opportunity."

"I've decided to stay in my job in Knotlington," Owen said. "I can't really think now why I ever thought of going away."

"Because that's what you want to do, isn't it?"

"But Caroline doesn't much want to."

"It's strange, but the first time I met the two of you, I thought she was as excited about the prospect as you were."

"We hadn't thought things over yet."

Andrew gave a regretful shake of his head. "It seems a pity. How long have you got before you've absolutely got to commit yourself, or have you done that already?"

"D'you mean, have I told the people in London I've decided against going? No, I haven't done that yet, but I'll write to them tomorrow."

"Have you got to do it tomorrow? Can't you put it off for a little longer?"

Owen gave Andrew a puzzled look. "I suppose I can, but why should I?"

If Owen had come alone to the Royal Midland Andrew would probably have told him, but he lacked the courage to do it with Caroline there to hear him.

"It's just that I think it would be wise to give yourselves a little longer to think it over," he said. "I know how difficult it can be. I did a good deal of moving around when I was young, and each time I'd go through a phase of being sure I was making a fearful mistake. And once or twice, of course, I was. But the great thing is to give yourselves time to think the matter over very carefully. Even for a few days. Don't do anything in a hurry."

"I can see that it may make sense," Owen said uncertainly. "Anyway, it can't do any harm. I only wish I understood why you're so keen about it."

"There's no need to go into that. Say it's just that I feel a certain responsibility. . . . Just give yourselves a little time before you cancel anything, then you may understand what I've been talking about. And if you still want to stay here, of course it's up to you. Only I think you may decide you want to go. How long is it before you actually have to leave?"

"About a month."

"That isn't very long, but you'll have made up your minds long before that, I imagine."

"We've made up our minds now," Caroline said. "There's no need to go on and on about it. We've talked it over and we know what we've got to do and that's to stay here. I can't leave my mother to look after herself. It isn't as if my parents can afford to move into one of those really good private homes where she'd be properly looked after, or to have a housekeeper living in, even supposing they could find such a person. And my father will be retiring soon and having to manage on his pension. So I told Owen I'd simply got to stay. He tried to argue me out of it, but he came round to my point of view in the end and said he'd

give up the idea of the job in Canada. It was a very good job and
I know it's a sacrifice and it means a lot to me that he's ready to
make it, so there you are—it's all decided and there's no need for
us to go on arguing about it."

"A few days—just wait a few days before you cancel anything."

Andrew felt pressure building up insided him to go on and
say far more and he controlled it only with some difficulty. A
part of the difficulty was that he was not really sure that it was
right to control it. Would it have been better to warn these two
young people who seemed to be very much in love, and at the
same time to have a rather moving sense of obligation to others,
that in all probability they had a shock coming to them, a far
worse shock than anything that they could ever have imagined?
Would a warning help them?

Probably not, because they would not believe him. He stood
up, saying he had only wanted to help and he hoped that they
would forgive him for his interference; then he made his way
out of the hotel to the street and started the walk back to Giles's
flat.

He found that Margaret was still there and that she and Giles
were settled with drinks in what looked a very comfortable do-
mestic fashion. Giles offered Andrew sherry, his usual drink,
but for once Andrew asked for whisky. As soon as he had sat
down, holding the glass, a sense of overpowering exhaustion
came to him. Apparently it showed, for Giles looked concerned.

"Are you all right, Andrew?" he asked. "You're a queer colour."

"Yes, yes, quite all right," Andrew answered. "It's only the
after-effects of doing one of the most difficult things I've ever
had to do in my life. A quite horrible thing. I've been talking to
two young things who ought to be left in peace to enjoy their
happiness and all the time I could see that bloody Sword of
Damocles hanging over their heads and knew it was going to fall
on them. And I did my best to tell them to get up and run for it

before that happened, but as I hadn't the courage to tell them why, naturally they didn't listen to me."

"You're talking about Caroline and Owen, are you?" Margaret said.

"Yes."

"But what's this about a sword?"

"It's simply the information that Caroline's father is a murderer," Andrew said, "and her mother's a blackmailer. A failed blackmailer, I admit, because her victim killed himself without paying anything, but when the news breaks, as I suppose it will in a day or so, those two kids will be glad if there's a bolt-hole waiting for them. Not that they'll go at once. They'll stay to give all the help they can. But then it'll be much the best thing for them to be able to get away."

"I don't understand," Giles said, looking as if he thought that Andrew might have had one or two whiskies before he started back from the Royal Midland. "What are you talking about?"

"About a very small, unimportant thing," Andrew said. "An overhead conversation that I only started thinking about this morning. There's also the matter of a door that was locked, just as it usually was. You'd be wise, I think, Giles, to get in touch with your friend Barrymore and tell him to get a search-warrant and search the Ramsdens' house for the knife that killed Carl Judd."

# Eleven

ANDREW KNEW THAT, before Giles could be induced to do what he suggested, he and Margaret would have to be told a great deal more than that. They both sat staring at Andrew while he drank about half his whisky in a couple of gulps. It did not really help. The tiredness that had overcome him felt as if it was in his bones and the drink did not touch it. It appalled him that he would have to go on talking, would have to say a great deal, would probably have to argue to convince the two of them that he was talking sense.

He was not prepared for what Margaret said. "Your nephew Peter was right then. You do understand this sort of thing."

It was not the right time to protest that he did not, yet it was precisely what Andrew wanted to do.

Giles got up quietly and topped up Andrew's drink.

"Well, go on," Giles said.

"It goes back to my first morning here," Andrew replied.

"I've been puzzled why Robert Hooke has been much more on my mind than usual, but it was simply because I spent that morning in the library, reading up some very interesting material they have about him. There were two people in the alcove next to the one I was sitting in. They were talking quietly and I didn't pay much attention to them till suddenly I heard one of them say distinctly, 'Remember, all the same, I've got the knife.' I know it was a strange thing to hear, but I didn't really pay it any attention. I was pretty absorbed in what I was doing and I hardly thought about it. Then one of the people got up and left and only a few minutes later Ramsden appeared and talked about my going to dinner with him and his wife. I hadn't identified the voices of the people who'd been talking, but later it dawned on me that they'd been Walter and Marriott. And Ramsden confirmed later that they'd been there together, but didn't mention what I only realized this morning, that he could have overheard at least as much as I had and probably a good deal more. He must have been as close to them as I was to have emerged to talk to me when he did, and something about them must have made him listen to them. If perhaps Walter had a way of paying off Marriott in the library, Ramsden may have noticed them meeting there and thought it a little odd and so decided to eavesdrop. And what he heard was Marriott reminding Walter of the hold he had over him because he'd got the knife that killed Judd and which Walter believed, rightly or wrongly, had his fingerprints on it, and so he'd better go on paying. And it happened, you see, that Ramsden had suddenly discovered that he needed money. Something had happened—all along I've had the feeling that something special must have happened to start all these other things happening, so long after Judd's death—and it had. It was the engagement of Caroline and Owen, and Owen's decision to accept the offer of the job in Toronto."

It seemed to Andrew that he had heard his voice going on and on for far too long, yet he had not come to the end of what he had to say. But he paused, and looked with some dismay at how much whisky had gone from his glass.

Both Giles and Margaret were watching him intently, waiting for him to go on.

When he did not do so, Margaret said, "You said something about a door that was locked as usual. What do you mean?"

"It was Walter's door," he answered. "What I think happened is this. Alison Ramsden phoned Walter sometime earlier in the day and told him she wanted to see him. Perhaps he was surprised, I don't know, but I believe he was a fairly good friend of hers so it wouldn't have seemed too strange, and they arranged that she should call on him in the evening. He told his housekeeper to put a tray ready with biscuits and so on, for him to make coffee when Alison arrived. And she phoned for a taxi and went to Walter's, and told the driver to wait for her to take her home again. It was all completely in the open, because that would be really less suspicious than being furtive. Yet she was in the house only about twenty minutes, which is rather a short time for a social call, but it might have been long enough for something to be settled. In other words, for her to tell Walter why she had come and for him to tell her that he did not intend to pay any blackmail and that she was to get out of his house. I think it must have taken her badly by surprise. She knew he'd been patiently paying blackmail to Marriott and she wasn't anticipating any difficulty in getting him to pay her and Ramsden instead. She didn't realise how near Walter had been to suicide ever since the murder of Judd."

"You're talking about Alison Ramsden?" Margaret exclaimed on a note of protest. "She isn't like that. She's one of my best friends."

"What do most of us know about our best friends?" Andrew asked. "Every time some particularly horrible crime is committed and someone's charged there's a horde of people to say what a nice quiet fellow he was and how they never dreamt he had such propensities. And think of Alison Ramsden, a woman living in a kind of cage, imprisoned by her own infirmities. But at least the cage was comfortable and she'd settled down to accepting the frustrations of her life without too much distress. Then two things happened. Her daughter, on whom she depended very much for day-to-day help wanted to get married and go far away, and her husband came home from the library, telling her what he'd overheard there. And between them they thought out a neat scheme of how to get money. And they were going to need money if their unpaid help was going to leave them. The wages of a housekeeper come high and so does the cost of one of those good old people's homes which they may have considered as an alternative to the housekeeper. And Ramsden was going to retire, so their income was going to drop. And all they had to do to get the money, they thought, was commit just one murder."

"And get hold of a knife and put a little pressure on Greenslade," Giles said. "It might have worked if they hadn't misjudged him. But it's all very hypothetical, Andrew."

"That's why I suggest you should try this theory of mine out on Barrymore," Andrew said, "and get him to search the Ramsdens' premises for the knife."

"But why do you think Alison went to Greenslade's house to blackmail him?" Margaret asked. "She could have had all sorts of other reasons for going there."

"Yes, and I also thought for a time someone else might have gone to the house after Alison Ramsden had left and that it was that person who was the blackmailer," Andrew said. "But how had that person got in? We know from the housekeeper that the door was locked as usual when she came home, so the only way he or she could have got in would have been if Walter had opened the door himself. That isn't impossible, but I don't believe it. I think Alison Ramsden was the only visitor he had that night, and that accidentally, through not understanding the state he was in, she killed him. You see, whoever it was who tried to blackmail him knew that that was what Marriott had been doing, and the one person we can be sure did know that was Ramsden. There's another minor matter which may not be important but which may be worth considering. I had a talk with Ramsden the other day in which he tried to find out how much the police knew about Walter's death, and incidentally he dropped the remark that he thought the marriage of Caroline and Owen was off and that he thought that was a good thing. He said that neither of them was ready to give up anything for the other and that that didn't promise well for the future. But I found out this afternoon that Owen had decided to give up the very good job he'd been offered, so what strikes me about Ramsden's attitude is that he's been doing his best to stop the marriage. He and Alison were keen enough on it as long as they thought they had enough money to arrange things comfortably for themselves without their daughter, but after Walter's death they had second thoughts."

"Why didn't Walter name Alison as the blackmailer in his letter?" Margaret asked.

"Don't you think it may have been a kind of revenge, leaving them to struggle on without the money they need so much? But perhaps he simply didn't care. He wanted to confess his own guilt, that was the important thing for him that night. Anyway, he may have known he couldn't prove anything against the Ramsdens."

Margaret gave a deep sigh, shaking her head.

"I don't know whether or not I believe it," she said.

Andrew looked at Giles, "You don't believe it either?"

"I'm not sure," Giles said. "I'll put it to Barrymore tomorrow and see if he thinks there's a case for searching the Ramsdens' house for the knife."

"Good," Andrew said. "That's reasonable. I feel fairly certain they'll find it."

He had no special wish, however, to remain in Knotlington until they found it, as later he heard they did. Next morning he took the ten o'clock train back to London, and arriving as usual half an hour too early for it, he bought a copy of the *Financial Times* and settled down on a bench on the platform to read it. But while he did this, a thought kept nagging at his mind, distracting him. There was something that he ought to remember, something important. But his memory had become so unreliable these days that he was quite unable to grasp it.

He was half-away to London before he suddenly knew what it was. He was feeling drowsy, and the *Financial Times* had sunk onto the table before him. His eyelids had drooped. Then a rhyme began to take possession of his brain:

> *"Oh, where are you going to, all you Big Steamers,*
> *   With England's own coal, up and down the salt seas?"*
> *"We are going to fetch you your bread and your butter,*
> *   Your beef, pork, and mutton, eggs, apples and cheese. . . ."*

Cheese, that was it. That was what he had been trying to remember. He must not forget, he thought, when he was shopping later in the afternoon for food for his meal that evening, that he had run out of cheese.

But those lines were Kipling, not Longfellow. Kipling, for whom he had felt intense admiration at the age of twelve or thereabouts, had defeated Longfellow for the moment. The change was welcome. No doubt when that verse had been going round and round in his head for the next few days he would tire of it, but just then it gave him pleasure.

E. X. Ferrars, who lives in England, is the author of fifty works of fiction, including *Come to Be Killed, The Crime and the Crystal, Root of All Evil,* and *Something Wicked.* She was recently given a special award by the British Crime Writers Association for continuing excellence in the field of mystery writing.